NEW CASES FOR DR. MORELLE

Young heiress Cynthia Mason lives with her violent stepfather, Samuel Kimber, the controller of her fortune — until she marries. So when she becomes engaged to Peter Lorrimer, she fears Kimber's reaction. Peter, due to call and take her away, talks to Kimber in his study. Meanwhile, Cynthia has tiptoed downstairs and gone — she's vanished without trace. Her friend Miss Frayle, secretary to the criminologist Dr. Morelle, tries to find her — and finds herself a target for murder!

ERNEST DUDLEY
Edited by Philip Harbottle

NEW CASES FOR DR. MORELLE

Complete and Unabridged

LINFORD
Leicester

First published in Great Britain

First Linford Edition
published 2013

British Library CIP Data

Dudley, Ernest.
  New cases for Dr. Morelle. - -
(Linford mystery library)
1. Morelle, Doctor (Fictitious character)- -
Fiction. 2. Detective and mystery stories.
3. Large type books.
I. Title II. Series
823.9'14–dc23

ISBN 978–1–4448–1400–2

Published by
F. A. Thorpe (Publishing)
Anstey, Leicestershire

Set by Words & Graphics Ltd.
Anstey, Leicestershire
Printed and bound in Great Britain by
T. J. International Ltd., Padstow, Cornwall

This book is printed on acid-free paper

1

The Case of the Missing Heiress

It was early morning in London. A car was quickly threading its way through the traffic. As the car swung round a corner, the single woman passenger gazed anxiously out of the window, alternating with glancing at her watch.

At length the car drew up at the kerb outside a house in Harley Street.

Miss Frayle jumped out hastily, paid the driver and hurried up the steps. She winced slightly as she read the name on the plate by the front door: DR. MORELLE.

She opened door with her key, and hurried into the hall. She was an attractive, rather ingenuous looking blonde in her middle twenties. Clearly flustered, she whipped off her hat, and quickly gathered her hair into a bun, pinning it in position. Then she took out of her handbag a pair of thick-rimmed library spectacles, put them on and approached a door in the hallway.

As she knocked, she braced herself for an unpleasant reception,

Doctor Morelle's study was a very large room, high-ceilinged and almost completely lined with glass-fronted bookshelves filled with medical books in several languages.

The doctor's desk was a huge mahogany one. A smaller, typist's desk in the other corner served for Miss Frayle. Against the inner wall was the usual relaxing couch of the psychiatrist.

Miss Frayle entered the familiar room timidly, almost on tiptoe. Instantly a deep, authoritative voice assailed her:

'My dear Miss Frayle, if I were to observe that I am even remotely interested in whatever laboured form of excuse you are about to offer for your lateness, it would be an over-statement.'

'I'm most terribly sorry. I . . . '

'I gather from the reek of glandular extract from the civet cat, coupled with the unnatural glossiness of your hair that you consider a permanent wave more important than transcribing my case-book!'

As usual, Miss Frayle withered under his fire.

'But, doctor, I . . . '

'Humanity, Miss Frayle, will not agree with you. Kindly fetch your notebook and begin to take my dictation.'

Doctor Morelle was lean, with a high forehead, and shrewd piercing eyes. A pompous studied manner underlined the natural grace of a man who had been European Fencing Champion for three successive years. With controlled impatience, his eyes followed Miss Frayle as she went to her desk to fetch her notebook and pencil.

He selected a cigarette from a box, leaned back in his chair and reflectively sent a puff of smoke ceilingwards as she seated herself near to his desk.

'We will call this next episode the Case of the Missing Heiress. It is chiefly remarkable for the fact that my assistant, Miss Frayle, featured prominently in it . . . '

Miss Frayle alerted with flattered excitement.

'... and by her entirely inept efforts hampered me considerably in arriving at the solution of the problem.'

Miss Frayle relapsed into disappointment.

'... Barren Tor, as its name suggests, is situated in the West Country. It is a lonely and isolated mansion, two miles from the nearest village, three from a Railway Station, and far removed from any bus route. To reach the house, you turn off the main Exeter Road at Gibbett Corner ... so-called from the bodies of Monmouth's rebels, which used to dangle here in chains when the notorious Judge Jeffreys stayed at Barren Tor for the Assizes ...'

Miss Frayle gave a little shudder as she recalled the events of the case. Her pencil began to press a little harder onto the notepaper.

'... There is a drive nearly half a mile in length leading to the north front of the house, behind which, on the evening of October 15th, at about seven o'clock the

4

curtain is rising on the grim drama of Cynthia Mason . . . '

★ ★ ★

Samuel Kimber, Cynthia's stepfather, was seated by the fire in his wheelchair. He was an unpleasant man, of schizoid tendencies, whose lack of self-control was only equalled by his dictatorial attitude to his stepdaughter.

Cynthia was seated with him in his study, an expression of anger and dismay crossing her face as she listened to him. Abruptly she got to her feet.

'I've heard enough! I'm leaving!'

Kimber gesticulated angrily as Cynthia made to leave the room.

'Cynthia!' he shouted. 'Where do you think you are going? Come back — do you hear me? Come back at once!'

The distraught girl ignored him and swept out of the room.

Kimber's manservant Bensall appeared in the doorway through which Cynthia had departed.

'Come back!' Kimber yelled after her.

'Do as you're told! Come back here!' He glared at Bensall.

'Follow her, Bensall. See what she's up to, the little fool.'

Bensall, his face expressionless, gave a slight nod, turned, and closed the door.

Outside, Cynthia hurried down the drive. It was almost pitch black, the gloom only slightly alleviated by the light coming from a couple of windows where there was a chink in the curtains. Fearfully, she glanced over her shoulder, and stopped as an owl hooted dismally.

The moon appeared from a break in the clouds and its pale light picked out her distraught face, while the shadow of branches swaying in the wind passed across it.

Tense with fear and anxiety, she stood listening intently. She could distinctly hear the sounds of someone making their way through the undergrowth.

With a muffled exclamation of fear, Cynthia turned and started running.

She ran desperately into the night, moving swiftly along familiar paths. After what seemed an eternity, but was actually only a few minutes, she came to a small two-storey cottage.

She gave a little gasp of relief as she saw a light in the downstairs window where the curtains had not been completely drawn. Breathing hard, she stumbled up to the front door, gasping for breath.

Inside the cottage, Peter Lorrimer, a dark-haired, good-looking but weak-faced young man was seated at his desk, writing.

At the thunderous knock on the door, he rose and crossed the room to the door.

He opened the door to admit Cynthia, who staggered in, pushed the door shut and leaned against it.

'Cynthia!' he exclaimed.

'Oh, Peter . . . ' she panted. 'Oh, Peter . . . I'm so . . . frightened . . . I had to come to . . . you!'

'Darling! What's frightened you?'

'It's my stepfather. He's getting worse and worse.'

'Has he been shouting at you again?' Peter patted her hand.

'I tried to tell him . . . about us . . .

wanting to get married . . . but he started screaming at me . . . one of these days he'll kill me, Peter!'

'Nonsense, darling. You're all upset!'

Cynthia shook her head. 'It's true, Peter. It's the money, Peter. He just can't face paying out my inheritance.'

Peter frowned. 'But he's got to . . . by law . . . now that you are 21 . . . it's in your mother's will.'

'He won't do it. He'll kill me first. That's why I told him tonight . . . '

She broke off and turned away. Peter followed her, gripped her arms gently so that she faced him again.

'Told him what?'

'That if he'd give his consent to our getting married, he could keep the money. I wouldn't claim it. All I want is you, Peter . . . I love you. I don't care how poor we are . . . '

Peter moved his grip and hugged her shoulders. 'I couldn't let you do that, darling. I can't support you. My writing barely brings in anything yet. There must be some other way.'

'There isn't any other way,' Cynthia

said dispiritedly. 'I daren't go back to him. Take me away, Peter. To London . . . anywhere . . . then perhaps he'll leave us in peace.'

'But, dear, you've got nothing with you!' Peter pointed out. 'We can't go off leaving him all your possessions into the bargain!'

Cynthia handed him an envelope. 'I've brought these. It's mother's will and mine, and my papers . . . I didn't want him to get these . . . '

Peter went to his desk, and quickly looked through the papers. At length he put the papers down on the desk, and stood for a moment, lost in thought. Then he crossed back to her.

'Listen, darling, I'll tell you what we'll do. You go back to the house — '

Cynthia interrupted him. 'I daren't, I'm too frightened!'

Peter ignored her words and went on: ' — and tell your stepfather I'm coming to see him, this evening, in an hour. While you're doing that I'll pack a bag, and get the car out and come round to the gates at the bottom of the drive. I'll leave the car there and come up to the house.'

'But supposing he refuses to see you?'

'He'll see me all right.' Peter was confident. 'Directly I'm with him, run upstairs, pack a bag, put all your valuables in it and get out of the house without being seen, and down to the car.'

'But if you're there, why can't I wait for you?'

'In case I fail. I'm going to take you away, darling, whatever happens. But at any rate, we'll put up a fight for your inheritance!'

Cynthia threw her arms round his neck.

'Oh, Peter, nothing else matters to me — only you!'

'And you know it's the same with me, my sweet!' He kissed her softly. 'Now, hurry, darling. We haven't a moment to lose. Only an hour, and then we'll be together — always.'

He took her to the door and opened it. A shaft of light shone out from the open door as Cynthia moved off into the darkness, while Peter remained in the doorway, looking after her. Suddenly he tensed as he caught sight of an approaching figure, a sinister silhouette against the light from the doorway. Peter stepped forward

'Who's there? Who's that?'

'It's only me,' came the voice of Bensall.

'Bensall!' Peter was surprised. 'What are you doing here?'

'Taking my dog for a walk.'

Peter looked down and frowned in puzzlement. 'Dog?'

'Yes, sir. At my heels — as he always is.'

'There's no dog there.'

'How logical you are, sir,' Bensall smiled strangely. 'To me he is always there. The best friend I ever had. I always take him for a walk about this time. It's become a habit, although it's fifteen years since he died. Goodnight, sir.'

As Bensall moved off into the darkness, he looked back with a quizzical half-smile. Peter stared at him for a moment, tight-lipped and suspicious. Then he shrugged and went back into the house and shut the door.

Returning to the living room, Peter

crossed to the desk and picked up Cynthia's papers, and began to look through them again.

* * *

Kimber and his stepdaughter were sitting at a table laid for supper. The room in which they sat was luxuriously furnished, indicating that Kimber was evidently a man of excellent, and expensive, taste.

Cynthia, white and trembling, was cowering back in her chair, looking across at Kimber — waiting, terrified for his reaction to the news she had just told him.

Kimber's reaction was unexpected; his face was sad, brooding — almost gentle.

'My dear, you make me very sad. That you are not happy here with me I have sensed for a long time. There is little in this house to interest a young girl . . . '

Cynthia blinked in amazement. She had expected his reaction to be one of violent rage.

' . . . but I had pictured things

12

happening differently. I had hoped that I should be able to share in your happiness — plan with you for your future — advise you — but now you want to leave at once, in the middle of the night. Leaving me here to fend for myself . . . a helpless cripple . . . after all I've done for you, all these years . . . '

Bensall approached the table and placed a dish of meat in front of Kimber, who looked up at him mournfully.

'Bensall — Miss Cynthia wishes to leave us tonight.'

'Yes, sir.'

'You are sorry, aren't you, Bensall?'

'Yes, sir.'

'We shall be two lonely old men without her, Bensall.'

'Yes, sir.' Bensall placed the plates on the table and moved away towards the door.

Kimber lowered his head and began carving the meat. Suddenly he looked up and shouted after his manservant:

'Bensall, you've cooked this meat too much, you fool!'

Bensall turned and looked over his

shoulder without expression, then continued on his way. At this, Kimber's face distorted with rage.

'I like my meat bloody — you know that!' Suddenly he hurled the carving knife he was holding.

The knife struck the doorpost by Bensall's side and fell at his feet. He stooped and picked it up, fondling the knife for a moment.

'I will fetch a clean knife, sir,' he said imperturbably, and went out, shutting the door quietly after him.

* * *

Kimber pushed his plate aside. His gaze pinned his stepdaughter, who looked at him apprehensively from the other side of the table.

'What time did you say this young man was coming?' The gentleness, the crocodile tears had now gone from his voice. His manner was highly-strung, arrogant.

'Half past eight,' Cynthia said quietly.

'And his name?' Kimber asked sharply.

'Peter Lorrimer.'

'And he writes, you say?' Kimber tightened his lips. 'Writes what? Novels? Nonsense about romantic young men with no money who want to marry wealthy and attractive young women?'

Cynthia seemed on the point of tears at his withering sarcasm, and seeing this, Kimber changed his tone to a more ingratiating one:

'Cynthia, when you marry, you'll be a rich woman, whereas I shall then become a poor man.'

'But I told you,' Cynthia protested. 'I . . . '

'I've always tried to do my duty by you, and I shall continue to do it,' Kimber cut in. 'That's why I shall view this young man with a careful and a prejudiced eye.'

Cynthia got to her feet. She seemed on the point of saying something, then changed her mind and instead hurried from the room, narrowly missing Bensall, who was hovering in the doorway, Impassively he moved to one side to permit her exit from the room. Then he moved forward as Kimber signalled to him.

'Clear this mess away,' Kimber said sourly. 'I've lost my appetite.'

Bensall began clearing away, using the dinner trolley.

'I don't want to be disturbed,' Kimber told him imperiously. 'There's a young man, a Mr. Lorrimer coming. Let him in and then go to bed. Do you understand?'

'Yes, sir.'

* * *

The front door bell rang. Bensall, hovering expectantly, glided across the hallway and opened the door to reveal Peter Lorrimer standing outside.

'Good evening, sir,' Bensall murmured.

'Good evening,' Peter responded. 'Mr. Kimber is expecting me. Mr. Peter Lorrimer.'

Bensall nodded. 'Very good, sir. If you'd mind waiting a moment, I'll inform him.'

Bensall turned and, with a dignified tread, crossed the hallway to Kimber's study. Peter took a few steps forward, and gently closed the door behind him. Then he waited, looking about him.

As he looked up, he saw Cynthia leaning over the banister at the top of the stairs.

'Peter!' she whispered anxiously.

He made a little sign of encouragement. 'Don't worry, darling.'

Peter turned as Bensall reappeared from the study.

'This way, sir,' the servant murmured. He opened the study door, and motioned to Peter to go inside.

'Mr. Lorrimer, sir,' Bensall announced.

'Go to bed, Bensall.' Kimber glared at his servant dismissively.

'Yes, sir,' Bensall assented, imperturbable as ever. Then he withdrew from the room, closing the door carefully behind him,

Kimber fixed his gaze on Peter as he stood just inside the door.

'Come and sit here, Mr. er — Lorrimer.'

'Thank you.' Peter seated himself on the chair Kimber had indicated.

Kimber continued his appraising stare, then said: 'You want to marry my stepdaughter, Mr. Lorrimer?'

'I do, sir.' Peter said levelly.

'How long have you known Cynthia?'

Peter hesitated, then: 'About two or three months.'

'An unorthodox courting, Mr. Lorrimer. I have only learned of your existence this evening.'

Peter moistened his lips. 'You see, Mr. Kimber . . . '

'I do see!' Kimber snapped. 'It is only fair to tell you — what you have probably already observed — that my stepdaughter is a very highly-strung girl. Not to put too fine a point on it, she suffers from certain delusions.' Kimber paused, studying Peter's rather strained expression.

'Do I appear a very terrifying person to you, Mr. Lorrimer?'

'Well, sir, I . . . ' Peter's voice trailed off uncertainly.

'Do I appear to you to be the kind of person deliberately to make unhappy the only person I have left in the world since my wife's death?'

'I only know what I've been told.' Peter said flatly.

Kimber smiled twistedly. 'Cynthia, let us face it, suffers from a moderate degree of persecution mania.'

'Whatever she suffers from, I'm not going to let her give up her inheritance,' Peter said stiffly.

When Kimber spoke again, it was in a complete change of tone. 'And when do you propose that this marriage shall take place?'

'As soon as possible.' Peter tightened his lips. 'I'm taking Cynthia to London tonight.'

'Tonight?' The crocodile tears had come back into Kimber's voice. 'You will appreciate this comes as rather a shock to me, Mr. Lorrimer.' Kimber made a steeple of his fingers and as he leaned forward, the light caught his diamond ring.

'A great shock,' Kimber resumed. 'I am a sad and lonely man. It needs thinking about, Mr. Lorrimer . . . it needs talking about . . . Sit back, Mr. Lorrimer. Relax. Let's talk this over.'

★ ★ ★

Cynthia, dressed for travelling, and carrying a suitcase, tiptoed down the stairs and paused to listen outside Kimber's study door. His voice was faintly audible, but the words were indistinguishable to the anxious girl. Making up her mind suddenly, she crossed to the front door, opened it and went out into the darkness.

★　★　★

' . . . and that was the last that was seen of Cynthia Mason!'

Doctor Morelle permitted himself a sardonic smile as he paused in his dictation to Miss Frayle. 'She was not in Lorrimer's car when he went down to the gates at the conclusion of his interview with Samuel Kimber. And although he is reported to have searched for her the whole night through, he found no trace of her. Nor apparently could her stepfather throw any light on her whereabouts. Did she go to London after all? But then, why didn't she communicate with the one friend who was entirely within her confidence — Miss Frayle?'

Miss Frayle, her pencil poised over her notebook, felt a little shiver of pleasure at again being mentioned, and eagerly awaited his next sentence.

But his next words came like a douche of cold water.

'Had Miss Frayle's mental equipment equalled her impetuous anxiety, a great deal of trouble might have been saved. But, alas, that is far from the case . . . '

Miss Frayle bridled with indignation, but bit her lip.

' . . . She proceeded to adopt a course of action that can only be described as sheer imbecility.'

This was more than even Miss Frayle could stand.

'Dr. Morelle! I must . . . '

'Quiet, please.' Dr. Morelle commanded. 'Any interruption disturbs the flow of my thoughts . . . '

He began to resume his dictation, and as Miss Frayle jabbed viciously at her notebook, she broke the point of her pencil with an audible snap.

Dr. Morelle looked up, frowning. 'Take another one!'

Sulkily Miss Frayle selected another pencil from the container on her desk.

' . . . Instead of reflecting that the sensible course would have been to consult me immediately,' Dr. Morelle resumed, 'she decided to play the role of private detective, for which she is so patently ill-equipped, and spend some ten days' leave that was due to her, investigating the fate of Cynthia Mason on the spot. Starting from Paddington Station . . . '

★   ★   ★

Miss Frayle was clearly in a state of fluster as she emerged from the ticket office at Paddington Station. She had placed her ticket in her mouth, whilst holding her open handbag in one hand and a suitcase in the other.

Jostled by the crowd of people milling about the busy station, she tried vainly without hands to get the ticket out of her mouth into the handbag. In desperation, she put down the suitcase, but just as she was transferring the ticket to the hand-bag, a hurrying passerby bumped into her, and the contents of the bag were spilled all over the ground.

Quickly diving amongst the hurrying feet, Miss Frayle somehow managed to retrieve her property. Closing the bag, she started to hurry off, having left her suitcase behind. Fortunately she was stopped in the nick of time by an alert fellow traveller, who had been observing her antics with some amusement.

Blushing, Miss Frayle smiled her thanks, and grabbing the suitcase, hurried off towards the platform from which her Great Western Area Express train was shortly to depart.

She had barely settled into her seat when the train began to move off. Ruefully she reflected that had it not been for the courtesy of one of her fellow travellers, she might well have missed the train. She would, of course, have soon realized that she had left it behind, but in the time taken to retrieve it, her train would have left without her.

Which would undoubtedly have saved both her and Dr. Morelle considerable jeopardy in the days to come. But, as she sat in the speeding train, Miss Frayle's real anxiety over her missing friend's fate obscured any possible appreciation of the difficulties and dangers into which her ill-considered impulse was precipitating her.

It was dusk before Miss Frayle's train reached her destination, a small village a few miles from Barren Tor. She made inquiries of the first local person she saw and as a result she eventually found herself waiting in a somewhat decrepit shelter waiting for the local bus that would, she was told, take her nearer to her destination.

Darkness was falling by the time the bus stopped at the cottages that marked the last outpost of local civilization.

Miss Frayle was its last passenger, and was about to descend, when the driver, a somewhat taciturn young man, appeared. He helped her with her suitcase.

'Here we are, miss.'

'How far is it to Barren Tor from here?'

'Two mile . . . '

Miss Frayle gave a horrified start. 'What — ?'

'Two mile,' the driver repeated stolidly.

'Can I get a taxi?'

The driver shook his head. 'No taxi.'

'Isn't there *any* means of transport at all?'

'Sam Price's 'ire car.'

'Where's that?' Miss Frayle asked eagerly.

'In the garridge. Big end's gone.'

Miss Frayle's face fell. 'Then how do I get there?'

The driver shrugged, 'Walk.'

'But I don't even know the way,' Miss Frayle said desperately.

'Straight up the moor road, and past the 'Red Lion'.' The bus driver pointed. 'Two mile.'

'Oh, dear. But . . . '

'You're not likely to meet no one on the road this time of day. Leastways, unless old Daft Georgie's on the bottle again.'

'Daft Georgie?' Miss Frayle faltered

'But 'e don't mean no 'arm, really.' The driver moved back to the driving seat of his bus. As he climbed in, he looked back over his shoulder at the disconsolate Miss Frayle, adding: ''E's a bit touched like, you see.'

As the bus drove off, Miss Frayle gave a long sigh, then, clutching her suitcase, started up the road. As she went, making the best speed she could, she constantly looked over her shoulder in the fast-fading light.

Night had fallen by the time Miss Frayle, dishevelled and panting, arrived at the gates to the mansion at Barren Tor. Putting down her suitcase, she tried ineffectually to open the gates. As she struggled, she suddenly froze as she thought she heard footsteps behind her. The footsteps drew nearer, and Miss Frayle turned her head bravely to meet her fate.

She saw a grey-haired old man holding a lighted lantern.

'There's a knack to that there,' the man said, not unkindly. 'Let me show you.' He reached across her to release the catch on the gate, as Miss Frayle shrank back.

'What are you frightened of?' he

demanded querulously. 'Anybody'd think I was Daft Georgie.'

'Aren't you Daft Georgie?' Miss Frayle faltered.

The old man looked at her indignantly. 'Do I look like him?'

'I'm afraid I don't know what . . . '

'I'm Old Jim, the village carter.'

Miss Frayle breathed an audible sigh of relief.

'I bring his parcels up,' Old Jim said.

Miss Frayle alerted. 'Mr. Kimber's, you mean?'

''Oo else?' Old Jim frowned. 'Not a friend of 'is, are you?'

'Er — no,' Miss Frayle said hastily.

Old Jim relaxed. 'Then I don't mind telling you . . . he's the meanest old basket this side of Timbucktoo.' His tone became sarcastic. 'Yes — nice, cheerful 'ousehold, this is. Old Kimber ready to fly off the handle at the drop of a 'at — old Bensall, the butler, creeping about like twopennorth of lor-luv-us . . . and now Miss Cynthia's gone.'

'Where's she gone to?' Miss Frayle asked hopefully.

The old man shrugged, 'Nobody don't seem to know, and nobody don't seem to dare ask questions.' He paused, his voice becoming confidential. 'But there's something as I can tell you.' He leaned across to Miss Frayle and prodded home his points with a podgy forefinger.

'What — what is it?'

'There's a lot of very funny rumours flying about. Lodging as I do at the 'Red Lion' I 'ears lots o' things. There's some as say that Miss Cynthia's better dead nor living in this house. Worked 'er like a slave 'e did, cos 'e never could keep no female staff, what with 'is tempers. Always trying new housemaids 'e is — but they never stop. There was a new one supposed to 'ave come this week — but she ain't showed up yet. I imagine she's 'eard about things and isn't 'avin' any.'

Old Jim straightened up and stretched himself, then with a gruff 'Goodnight', he moved off.

Miss Frayle pulled herself together and set off up the drive.

Reaching the front door Miss Frayle knocked lightly. After a short interval the

door swung slowly open.

Miss Frayle edged inside, looking about her timidly.

She started as a harsh voice suddenly addressed her.

'Who are you? What do you want here?'

Miss Frayle spun round.

The speaker was Kimber, and Miss Frayle saw that he was seated in a wheelchair, Bensall, his manservant, standing alongside him.

'Well — I — I — I've — er — well . . . '

Kimber cut short her stammering: 'Are you the new housemaid? What's your name? Amy?'

Miss Frayle, with a sudden flash of inspiration, decided to take advantage of Kimber's misapprehension as to her identity.

'Yes . . . yes!' she assented.

'About time,' Kimber said sourly. 'Servants seem to think they can do as they like these days. Are you strong? Can you cook? Can you mend clothes? Not afraid of work?'

'N-no, sir.' Miss Frayle wilted under the verbal onslaught.

'All right. Bensall will show you to your room.'

As Kimber returned to his study, the manservant came forward silently, and picked up Miss Frayle's suitcase. She followed him upstairs until they came to a room, which had formerly been the loft.

Entering after Bensall, Miss Frayle looked around her. It was a somewhat bare, strangely-shaped attic storey.

'It — rambles a bit, doesn't it?' Miss Frayle remarked uneasily.

The manservant nodded, and gave her a sidelong glance. 'Very strange house, miss, this. Feller who built it must have been — a little eccentric.'

'Er — yes,'

'Down here, miss,' Bensall said, and guided her down a short flight of steps leading to a door. He opened it and went inside, Miss Frayle timorously following.

Bensall put down her suitcase and stepped respectfully to one side to allow Miss Frayle to view the room.

In marked contrast to the luxury in Kimber's study the room was cheaply and dingily furnished with odds and ends of cheap furniture; an iron bedstead, a bamboo table, a pine washstand with a cracked basin. A rickety chair or two, and a chest of drawers completed the bedroom's meagre furnishings.

Miss Frayle looked round the room with a sinking feeling of dismay. She caught Bensall's eye on her.

'This is your room.'

'Thank you, Bensall. It's — it's lovely.'

As the manservant turned to go, Miss Frayle pulled herself together and raised a restraining hand.

She had resolved to begin her detective duties, her mind working furiously to imagine what Dr. Morelle would have done had he been in her shoes. She began to fire questions in a businesslike manner.

'How long have you worked here?'

'Many years now,' Bensall replied, somewhat morosely.

'How many are there in the household?'

'Mr. Kimber — me — and you.'

A distinct feeling of uneasiness crept over Miss Frayle, but she managed to retain her assumed bravado.

'What about the young lady? Er — someone in the village said there was a — er — a Miss Mason.'

'She isn't here any more.'

'Oh?' Miss Frayle forced herself to remain casual. 'Where's she gone?'

Bensall did not reply. He affected not to have heard the question.

Miss Frayle spoke more loudly, 'I said — what's happened to her?'

This time Bensall responded, slowly and reluctantly. His tone was sombre. 'Don't ask too many questions. It's much easier here if nobody asks questions.' He pointed to the bamboo table. 'There's a house telephone over there. Mr. Kimber will call up if he wants you.'

Before Miss Frayle could think of voicing the further questions that still chased in her mind, Bensall turned and went out, shutting the door behind him.

Immediately he was gone, Miss Frayle whipped off her hat, and threw it on the bed. Then she went over to the door, and pressed her ear against it. She listened to Bensall's footsteps going away.

Miss Frayle decided to waste no time

in continuing her detective work. Opening her handbag, she extracted a pair of gloves, and put them on.

Carefully opening the door, she crept out, tiptoeing through the shadowy loft.

Reaching a corridor, she proceeded along it until she reached what she took to be a bedroom door. She paused, and looked around her. There was nobody about. Cautiously, she turned the handle on the bedroom door, and found it unlocked. She went inside.

There was sufficient light from an uncurtained window for her to see fairly clearly. She gazed at a luxuriously furnished bedroom, with curtains and furnishings of gay chintz. Obviously — as she had hoped — this was Cynthia's bedroom.

Curiously, she moved slowly around the room, looking for she knew not what. She paused to examine a floral calendar, which had been given pride of place over the dressing table.

She picked it up, and saw an inscription in a sprawling handwriting. She could just make it out:

'To dear Miss Cynthia, with respectful good wishes for a Happy Xmas. Bensall.'

Replacing it carefully, Miss Frayle resumed moving slowly around the room, taking her time.

A second window alcove was curtained off. She moved forward and pulled the curtain aside.

She stifled the shriek that rose to her lips at the sight of a man standing there, staring at her intently.

It was Bensall!

Before she could scream Bensall jumped out from the alcove, grabbing her and covering her mouth with his other hand.

Miss Frayle's eyes revealed her terror. But Bensall's clamped hand across her mouth prevented her from giving voice to her scream.

'Keep quiet and you won't get hurt!' Bensall whispered fiercely. 'Nod if you understand.'

After a moment's consideration, Miss Frayle nodded, and Bensall released her, and stood back,

Miss Frayle staggered over to the

bedrail, and steadied herself against it.

'What are you doing here?' Bensall demanded, low-voiced.

'I — I — I — well, I . . . ' Miss Frayle was completely at a loss.

'I don't mean in this room,' Bensall said. 'I mean, *what are you doing in this house?*'

'Housemaid.' Miss Frayle gulped.

Bensall's eyes narrowed with disbelief. 'With *those* hands? And a genuine new housemaid who knew her job would really call the butler 'Mister'.'

'I — I . . . ' Miss Frayle continued to falter helplessly.

'Who *are* you?' Bensall demanded. 'The Police?'

Miss Frayle shook her head miserably.

'Have you come about *her*?' Bensall whispered fiercely.

'Who?'

'If he has hurt her . . . ' Bensall began muttering to himself. 'If he has hurt her . . . '

'*He*? You mean Mr. . . . Kimber?'

Bensall looked about him apprehensively. 'Ssh!' he hissed.

Miss Frayle was beginning to sense that the man was not her enemy. 'Have you asked him about Cynthia?'

''He' only tells you what he wants you to know,' Bensall growled. 'You don't ask 'Him' questions.'

'She was terrified of him,' Miss Frayle told him. 'I was her friend and she told me so . . . and he's got control of all the money — until she gets married.'

Bensall gave a grim nod. 'I know.'

'And this young man she wanted to marry?' Miss Frayle asked.

'Mr. Lorrimer?'

Miss Frayle nodded. 'Can't *he* throw any light on what happened?'

Bensall shook his head gloomily. 'He's as much in the dark as anyone. He never leaves his cottage now . . . I've never seen a man look so strange and ill.'

Miss Frayle had a sudden inspiration. 'Suppose that's all a bluff?' she suggested. 'Suppose Cynthia is hiding there . . . in his cottage . . . until she's of age and they can get married without her stepfather's consent?'

Bensall was unimpressed. 'If she was

there, she'd have let me know.'

'But, perhaps she daren't,' Miss Frayle persisted, 'in case her stepfather found out.' She was determined to pursue her theory. 'D'you know the way to Mr. Lorrimer's cottage?'

'Certainly,' Bensall affirmed.

'Then we'll go and see him now. Both of us.' Miss Frayle looked at Bensall appealingly. Judging by that calendar, she reasoned, he must be fond of the girl . . .

Under her imploring gaze, Bensall wavered, then agreed. 'But 'he' mustn't see us leave the house.'

'We'll slip out of the back door,' Miss Frayle breathed. 'Come along.'

She moved cautiously towards the door, and Bensall followed her. Suddenly. he turned and gave a low whistle and snapped his fingers.

Miss Frayle looked at him in blank astonishment.

Bensall glanced at her. 'You don't mind if I take my little dog, miss? He does so love a walk.'

Miss Frayle looked around the room in bewilderment. 'Your dog?'

'He'll be no trouble, miss.' Bensall smiled oddly, then as Miss Frayle looked at him in incipient alarm, he added:
'You see, he's dead!'

★ ★ ★

After managing to leave Kimber's house — apparently undetected — Miss Frayle followed Bensall through the night, with a distinct feeling of unease as he occasionally spoke to his invisible dog. She was thankful when at last they came to Peter Lorrimer's cottage.

Bensall approached the front door and knocked heavily.

No answer. Bensall knocked again, but without result.

Miss Frayle expelled a long sigh. 'He must be out . . . ' She looked at Bensall. 'Should we break in?'

Surprisingly, Bensall promptly agreed. 'Leave it to me.' He bent down, pulling a tool out of his pocket and inserted it in the lock. A few seconds later there came a distinct click, and the door swung open. As Bensall straightened, Miss Frayle found her courage and entered ahead of him.

The first room they searched was the living room, Bensall switching on the light.

Miss Frayle moved over to a large desk, and began desultorily looking through the papers on it.

Most of them appeared to be the manuscripts of some book Lorrimer was working on, but suddenly Miss Frayle gave an excited exclamation.

'Quick, Bensall, look!'

Bensall hurried across to her side. Miss Frayle brandished one of the documents she had been examining. 'It's a will! It's Cynthia's mother's will. I happen to know Cynthia always kept it with her, in case her stepfather destroyed it.'

Bensall looked at her keenly. 'You mean, Miss Cynthia must have brought it here?'

Before Miss Frayle could answer, there came the sound of a door opening.

Miss Frayle had the presence of mind to quickly put the document back where she had found it before the returning

Peter Lorrimer had entered the room.

He paused in astonishment as he saw the two intruders.

'Bensall, what are you doing in here?'

'Well, sir . . . '

As Bensall prevaricated, Miss Frayle jumped in: 'We were taking a walk and we decided to call on you.'

Peter looked at her with a frown. 'Who are you?'

The intervention had allowed Bensall time to gather his wits. 'Begging your pardon, sir, this is the new housemaid at Barren Tor.'

Peter's haggard face became suffused with suspicion. 'Mr, Kimber didn't send you to spy on me?'

'Good gracious, no!' Miss Frayle declared.

Peter came into the room, shaking his head. 'I wouldn't put anything past him. He's at the bottom of Cynthia's disappearance, you mark my words.'

Peter sank wearily into a chair, and rested his forehead on his hand. He remained slumped in the chair, not speaking.

Miss Frayle, who had been expecting a barrage of irate questions as to how they had entered his house, realized that the man had so much on his mind that he appeared to have no concern as to their illegal entry. She stepped forward, determined to tackle Peter about the will.

But just as she was opening her mouth to speak, Bensall again interposed:

'Come along, Amy!'

As Miss Frayle looked at him in astonishment, Bensall took her arm firmly and continued:

'You can see the gentleman clearly doesn't want to be disturbed. We'll call some other time.'

Bensall led Miss Frayle from the room, and out of the front door of the cottage. He closed the door carefully, then turned as Miss Frayle touched his shoulder.

'Bensall . . . listen!' she said eagerly. 'Cynthia must have gone to the cottage otherwise how could her mother's will have got there?'

Bensall shrugged. 'She was there the evening she disappeared, miss — she could have brought it then.'

41

Miss Frayle wrinkled her brow. 'Yes, that's true. But what harm would it have done, if I'd told him who I was and asked him about her?'

Bensall took her arm, moving off in the direction of Barren Tor. 'I think it best, miss, if, for the moment, we keep your identity secret. Now come on, it's late. We must get back before Mr. Kimber discovers our absence.'

★   ★   ★

The next morning found Miss Frayle in the kitchen, trying to maintain her assumed identity as Amy, the hired maid. She was still wearing the stylish visiting dress she had on when she had arrived at Barren Tor, but was seeking to protect it with a large apron.

She was evidently attempting to prepare some kind of egg dish for lunch.

She deposited an armful of ingredients, including a bag of flour, a small bowl of eggs, a jug of milk, and measuring jar on the kitchen table by the side of a huge mixing bowl.

Next, she poured some fat into a large frying pan, standing well back so that it didn't splash her dress. Placing the pan on the stove, she then began to crack eggs into the bowl. To her dismay, the first one fell outside the bowl, the second all the way on to the floor, and whilst she succeeded in getting the third one into the bowl, it had retained half its shell.

'Butter,' she muttered to herself, carelessly taking the wrapper from a half-pound packet and tossing it whole into the bowl.

'Flour next . . . '

She took a large paper bag of flour and began carefully tipping some into the bowl.

Suddenly the fat in the frying pan caught fire.

Alarmed, Miss Frayle spun round, upending the paper bag so that all the flour fell in a deluge all over the table and floor. In desperation, she seized a jug of milk and began pouring it into the frying pan to put out the flame, causing clouds of smoke.

Bensall was watching from the doorway, shaking his head sadly.

Somehow Miss Frayle succeeded in dousing the flame, then she saw Bensall regarding her lugubriously.

She surveyed the mess she had made and smiled at him apologetically.

'I think I'd better start again, don't you?' she said brightly.

Bensall gave a silent nod, watching as Miss Frayle began to gather a new set of ingredients. He was about to say something when there came a harsh shout from somewhere in the distance.

'Bensall!' Kimber was calling irritably. 'Bensall!'

Moments later the kitchen door was pushed open, and Kimber entered in his wheelchair. He glared at his manservant.

'Bensall, why hasn't my room been done?'

'Amy's just going up to do it now, sir,' Bensall said hastily.

With a snarl Kimber turned to Miss Frayle, who backed away, terrified.

'You lazy little slut! If you don't get down to your work, out you go!' His eyes bulged, and saliva flecked his curling lips. 'D'you understand me, you — you — dough-faced dancehall blonde!'

This verbal onslaught was too much even for Miss Frayle, whose terror was overcame by her anger at his words.

'I *won't* be . . . '

Bensall quickly intervened, grabbing her arm. *'Don't!'* he whispered

'Get upstairs at once!' Kimber shouted. 'Do you hear?'

Biting her lip, Miss Frayle hurried out, followed by Bensall.

Kimber looked at the mess on the floor with narrowed eyes, then gripped the wheels of his chair and went out also.

As Miss Frayle entered Kimber's bedroom she was seething with anger. Her usual diffidence had evaporated. She turned her head to look at Bensall, following close behind her.

'How dare he speak to me like that?' she demanded.

'At all costs, don't cross him, miss,' Bensall counselled. 'There's no knowing what he might do to you in one of his rages.'

45

Miss Frayle hesitated, clenching her fists. Then Bensall's earnest advice had a sobering effect. She turned and began to make the bed, Bensall dexterously assisting.

'He's responsible for Cynthia's disappearance!' Miss Frayle said, breathing hard. 'I feel it in my bones he knows all about it. After all, all the money remains in his hands if . . . '

'Don't say it, miss!' Bensall implored. 'It doesn't bear thinking of.'

But Miss Frayle had now been struck by another thought. Dropping her side of the blanket, which they were pulling up, she dashed to the wardrobe. She flung it open, disclosing Kimber's suits hanging inside.

Miss Frayle began 'frisking' the pockets of the suits, as Bensall stood watching nervously. 'What are you doing?' he asked.

'Searching for a clue . . . '

'But . . . what sort of a clue?'

'I don't know,' Miss Frayle admitted, continuing her desperate search. 'But Dr. Morelle — er — a man I know says you'll always find clues to where a man has been — in his wardrobe. Bus tickets in a pocket, a woman's hair on a jacket, dust on his shoes . . . '

Bensall frowned. 'Well, you know perfectly well Mr. Kimber hasn't been anywhere. He can't get out of the house except in his chair, and that he hardly ever does.'

Miss Frayle was unfazed by this logic. 'Never mind. We may find some sort of clue, and — '

She broke off suddenly and pointed to the bottom of the wardrobe.

A row of men's shoes were beautifully cleaned and polished, *except for one pair, which was covered with dust.*

'Look there!' Miss Frayle breathed. 'Dust on his shoes!' Her hand flashed down and picked up the dusty pair.

Peering through her thick lenses, she examined the shoes.

'It's ash,' she pronounced at length. 'And look — ' she indicated a suit hanging in the wardrobe — 'there's more in the turn-ups of this pair of trousers.'

Bensall looked wonderingly. 'Ash — and clay.'

Miss Frayle furrowed her brows. 'But where could it have come from?'

'I don't know, miss,' Bensall said slowly. 'Perhaps . . . perhaps from the incinerator in the outhouse . . . but he can't walk!'

'How do you know?' Miss Frayle demanded. 'You mean you haven't *seen* him walk. Come on!'

Bensall looked at her blankly. 'Where to?'

'The incinerator, of course — '

She started to move towards the door, but Bensall stopped her.

'We daren't go now, miss, not while *he's* about.'

'Then we'll wait until he's gone to bed.' Miss Frayle tightened her lips. 'Nothing's going to stop me having a look at that incinerator tonight.'

★　★　★

Two figures were moving furtively in the darkness. They stopped as they reached a narrow brick-built shed with a door at one end. Dimly discernible in the

48

moonlight was a brick oven against one wall.

The larger of the two figures reached out and pulled open a door, letting in the moonlight, which suffused one end of the shed.

Bensall and Miss Frayle advanced into the shed. Miss Frayle produced a small electric torch from her handbag and flashed it about. She moved over to the oven.

'Someone has been here,' she whispered, 'the ash has been scattered quite recently.'

Bensall bent over the oven. 'Look, some turf has been thrown in on top here — it's still green. Perhaps — '

He broke off abruptly at a sudden sound from outside. It was recognizable as approaching footsteps.

Miss Frayle and Bensall stared at each other in horrified silence.

Bensall made a sign to Miss Frayle to switch off her torch, and moved towards the door. At that moment, Miss Frayle, glancing frantically about her, noticed something amongst the ashes. Curiosity overcame her mounting fear and she bent to pick it up. Her hand closed on a sapphire earring. Her torchlight showed that the setting had been twisted and bent by the heat of the fire. She switched off her torch and crouched by the oven.

Suddenly there was a strangled groan from the door. Miss Frayle looked up.

In the doorway she saw a vague figure grappling with Bensall, silhouetted against the moonlight. The figure lifted an arm and struck downwards viciously.

Bensall gave a strangled groan and fell to the floor. The figure stooped over him for a moment, and then turned away, vanishing into the night.

Miss Frayle, frozen with terror, remained where she was, crouched by the oven. Long seconds passed. When the figure did not return, she pulled herself together and slowly moved towards the doorway.

Bensall was lying motionless where he had fallen. Gingerly Miss Frayle moved past him and looked cautiously out through the door. Seeing no one, she came back and fell to her knees beside

Bensall, pillowing his head in her lap.

'Bensall!' she gasped. 'Bensall!'

His eyes flickered open.

'Are you badly hurt?'

Bensall groaned.

Miss Frayle bent her head towards him. 'Who was it? Did you see?'

Bensall nodded, apparently unable to speak. Miss Frayle noticed that he was clutching at his breast.

Miss Frayle reached down and gently tore his shirt open. Her eyes widened in horror as she saw the extent of his wound. Immediately she tried to staunch the blood with her handkerchief, but she knew instinctively that the wound was a fatal one. She stared at him with tear-filled eyes.

'Who was it? Try to tell me.'

Bensall had fixed his glassy eyes on the ground by his side. Slowly his hand made a soft, caressing gesture.

'Little dog . . . look after . . . little dog.'

'Yes, yes, I will!' Miss Frayle promised. 'But tell me, who was it? Try to tell me.'

But Bensall made no answer. He suddenly became rigid; then his head fell to one side.

With a shudder of horror, Miss Frayle gently lowered him to the ground. She rose to her feet, and cautiously went out. But in doing so, she was unaware that she had dropped her blood-soaked handkerchief.

Somehow Miss Frayle managed to make her way back to the house. She had barely reached the back door, which they had left on a latch, when there was a vivid flash of lightning, followed by a low rumbling. A storm was breaking.

Risking her torch in short bursts, Miss Frayle made her way on tiptoe through the house. Reaching the hall telephone, she lifted the instrument with a trembling hand, and dialled for the Operator.

'I want a call to London, please,' she whispered. 'It's urgent ... Welbeck 74382. Reverse the charges ... '

* * *

Doctor Morelle was at home, in his shirtsleeves, practising fencing thrusts in a long mirror, when his telephone rang.

With a deep sigh, he dropped his foil

and went to his desk and picked up the telephone.

'Dr. Morelle speaking . . . will I accept a reversed charges call from where? I've never heard of it. Where is it? . . . Devonshire. I'm sorry, I know nobody in that vicinity. I do not accept the call . . . what name? . . . Frayle? I see, in that case, very well, but for three minutes only. Hello . . . '

When she heard the Doctor's voice Miss Frayle was almost hysterical with relief at having made contact. Desperately she restrained herself from almost shouting into the receiver.

'Oh, Dr. Morelle! . . . It's me . . . Miss Frayle . . . I'm in terrible trouble . . . I found Cynthia . . . but she's dead . . . '

With an expression of annoyance Dr. Morelle held the receiver away from his ear. The metallic sound of Miss Frayle's voice as she babbled on hysterically was clearly audible in the room.

'I found her earring . . . in a brick oven and Bensall, the butler, has been murdered . . . only a few minutes ago. We found ashes on his boots . . . he was kind . . . now I'm alone . . . '

Dr. Morelle broke in, his voice stern with exasperation: 'Miss Frayle! I insist you remain silent for the space of a minute . . . '

Miss Frayle had been conditioned by her long association with Dr. Morelle: the habit of obedience caused her to instantly remain silent, her mouth open as she listened to the doctor's sardonic voice.

' . . . and breathe in deeply through the nose, expelling through the mouth . . . '

Obediently, Miss Frayle proceeded to breathe in through her nose and gasp out through her mouth.

Dr. Morelle gave a sidelong glance at his fencing foil.

'It's bad enough to be distracted from my work, which is of — er — considerable scientific importance . . . but when it's to listen to some monstrous verbal phantasmagoria of charred bones, ashes on boots, and murdered butlers . . . '

His biting sarcasm was too much, even for Miss Frayle. She interrupted with weary earnestness:

'There's no time for all that stuff, Dr. Morelle. I'm desperate. Five minutes ago a man died in my arms . . . I'm in danger myself . . . real danger . . . you've just *got* to come and help me.'

At that instant Dr. Morelle realized that his secretary was being serious, and his manner changed to matter-of-fact practicality.

'Very well, Miss Frayle, I'll come by the midnight train, provided you do exactly as I tell you.'

'Yes, Dr. Morelle.'

'Write me a report of everything that's happened. Omit nothing, and embroider nothing. What is the nearest station to Barren Tor?'

'Moorminster,' Miss Frayle panted. 'It's three miles.'

'Have you anyone you could send there with your report?'

Miss Frayle furrowed her brow, then suddenly had a flash of inspiration. 'Yes — Old Jim! I can find him at the 'Red Lion'.'

'Good. Have him hand your manuscript — sealed, of course — to the stationmaster. I will collect it from him tomorrow morning and take whatever course I feel to be the most advisable under the circumstances. When you've finished handing over your report, go back to the house and go straight back to bed, and try and get some sleep. Try not to do anything stupid.'

Miss Frayle gave a gasp of dismay. 'Do I *have* to return here, Doctor?'

'Yes. It is essential to my investigation that your — er — employer does not suspect anything.'

'But — ' Miss Frayle protested faintly.

'In the event of criminal activity, which immediately threatens your own personal safety, communicate with the local Police Constabulary . . . or preferably lock your bedroom door . . . goodbye!'

Miss Frayle carefully replaced the receiver, and steeled herself for further efforts.

★ ★ ★

Miss Frayle closed and locked her bedroom door. A lightning flash lighted up the room. She gave a little shudder, thankful for the fact that the storm had abated during her journey to and back from the 'Red Lion'. But now it was starting up again.

As the thunder rumbled she wedged the door with a chair, and then proceeded to drag more furniture in the room against the door, making a barricade.

She breathed a sigh of relief, feeling that now she was adequately protected from Kimber.

As an afterthought she looked under the bed. Nothing there. She relaxed a little, looked again at the furniture barricade and drew solace from it.

Miss Frayle gave a start as the telephone rang suddenly.

She put out her hand, and hesitated, lacking the courage to lift the receiver. Then, as it continued to ring, she jerked up the receiver.

'Hello?' she whispered.

'Are you there?' Kimber's voice demanded.

'I'm perfectly all right. I'm very well, thank you.'

'Stop talking nonsense and listen,' Kimber snapped impatiently. 'You had better be up sharp in the morning.

57

Bensall has left . . . '

As Miss Frayle replaced the telephone, she felt a chill of fear. Bensall left? *How did Kimber know?*

A sudden loud clap of thunder sent her scurrying to the bed, where she covered herself with the bedclothes.

★ ★ ★

Dr. Morelle reached out a lean hand, and knocked authoritatively on the front door of Kimber's mansion.

It was a fine winter's day, and still early morning.

He was about to knock again, when the door half opened. Miss Frayle peered cautiously out, then, seeing who it was, she flung the door wide open. Her face beamed at him in relief and thankfulness.

Dr. Morelle placed a warning finger to his lips, then spoke in a low tone:

'Though flattered at my reception, it is essential you should pretend you don't know who I am from Adam. In other words, Miss Frayle, to use a distressing colloquialism, preserve the 'poker face', or, which should come naturally to you, the 'dead pan'.'

Miss Frayle was still euphoric. 'You don't know how much it means to see you — !'

Dr. Morelle waved a hand to cut her short. 'I've read your report — it's very interesting.' He looked at her and frowned. 'You look as if you didn't sleep well.'

'Oh, Doctor Morelle, I didn't. I was alone in the house with him last night,' — she jerked a thumb over her shoulder to indicate Kimber — 'I had all the furniture stacked against the door.'

With a nod of his head Dr. Morelle indicated that he wished to enter. He moved past her into the hall.

As Miss Frayle closed the door behind him, Dr. Morelle said loudly, 'Will you kindly inform your employer that Professor Harper would appreciate the privilege of a few words with him? My card.'

He presented his card to Miss Frayle who boggled for a moment, but pulled herself together quickly.

'Yes, sir. I'll tell him.' She moved off,

leaving Dr. Morelle standing in the hallway. Going to the door of Kimber's study, she knocked and entered.

Directly he was alone, Dr. Morelle made a rapid examination of the hall. He was just looking at the ferrule of a heavy walking stick which he had found leaning against the wall, when the door of the study opened, and Miss Frayle came out.

Immediately Dr. Morelle caught her by the arm and drew her aside. Leaning towards her he whispered urgently:

'Now pay attention. After I have been with Kimber a few minutes, come in with some news of a domestic crisis, that will make him come out with you for a minute or two, leaving me alone in there.'

Miss Frayle gulped and nodded vigorously. She pushed open the door of Kimber's study, and started to announce him:

'Doctor Mo — '

'*Professor Harper,*' Dr. Morelle cut in quickly. 'So kind of you to spare me a few moments, Mr. Kimber.'

He swept into the room past Miss

Frayle as she remained frozen, figuratively, biting her tongue off.

Kimber was sitting at his desk. On his left hand he was still wearing the heavy diamond ring as on the night of Peter Lorrimer's visit. Dr. Morelle noticed it as it glinted, and he saw too that the curtains were dawn over the windows, the room being lit by a strong desk-light.

Kimber came forward in his chair to meet Dr. Morelle.

Kimber had noticed the doctor's glance to the drawn curtains. 'Please forgive this somewhat bizarre lighting, but I've got into the habit of working by artificial light.'

'How interesting,' Dr. Morelle murmured. 'And how conducive to concentration.'

'Sit down, Professor,' Kimber invited. 'What can I do for you.'

Dr. Morelle seated himself opposite to Kimber, occupying the same chair that Peter Lorrimer had sat in on the fateful night that Cynthia had disappeared.

'Briefly, my mission is this,' Dr. Morelle began his prepared story. 'I have been invited by the County Historical and Topographical Society to prepare a paper on the old houses of the district. I wondered if you would be kind enough to give me some information about Barren Tor.'

'A reasonably full account of the house and its historical associations can be found in Riddal's 'Antiquities of Devon' — a work you doubtless know,' Kimber said.

'I do indeed, but its date of publication was 1827,' Dr. Morelle came back smoothly. 'I am sure there must be a great deal of interesting material of more recent date.'

Kimber shook his head. 'Virtually none, I assure you.' As he spoke, Kimber cupped his chin in his hands, in a characteristic attitude, and Dr. Morelle noticed his diamond ring catching the light.

'Riddal writes of some particularly fine carved panelling in the best bedroom,' Dr. Morelle went on. 'I would be very grateful for an opportunity of examining it.'

'I have neither the time nor the money

to keep this house in the state of preservation it warrants,' Kimber said flatly.

Dr. Morelle smiled thinly. 'Has anybody any money these days, Mr. Kimber?'

Kimber was watching Dr. Morelle closely. He leaned forward, his eyes shining in the light of the desk lamp. He turned the diamond ring round and round on his finger so that its facets kept catching the light.

'To a philosopher, money is immaterial,' he murmured.

'Yet even philosophers must eat, Mr. Kimber.'

Kimber leaned forward, staring directly into Dr. Morelle's eyes. 'It is surprising how little food they need, Professor. What a philosopher needs is — relaxation. To relax! That is the answer to the stress of modern life. Look at you! Tense and on edge! Relax, Professor, relax, and you will find . . . '

At that moment the door was flung open and Miss Frayle rushed in, in an assumed panic.

'Oh, sir! Do please come at once! The

boiler's bursting, sir. Steam is coming out, and it's boiling over and . . . Oh, sir! Do come, sir!'

She almost dragged a visibly annoyed Kimber from the room. Left alone, Dr. Morelle leapt into action. Going first to Kimber's desk, he pulled out each drawer, getting a quick idea of the contents. Once he gave a grunt of satisfaction and paused to note down an address.

Next he moved swiftly along the bookshelves glancing at the titles. He paused at one section with evident interest, muttering to himself in a pleased fashion. 'Really! Most interesting!' he muttered. 'Most interesting!'

He was standing in the middle of the room when the door was flung open and a very angry Kimber came back in.

'That girl's a fool!' he spat. 'I'll have to get rid of her. Nothing the matter with the boiler at all.' With a visible effort, he managed to control his temper. He turned to Dr. Morelle.

'Well Professor, I don't think we have anything more to say to each other.'

Dr. Morelle shrugged amiably; he had

accomplished his mission.

'No. I must be on my way. I've suddenly remembered a pressing appointment.'

Kimber glared at him suspiciously. 'What is it?'

Dr. Morelle gave a sardonic smile as he turned to the door.

'Not being a philosopher — lunch! Good day, Mr. Kimber.'

He went out into the hallway, leaving a thoroughly puzzled man staring after him.

Leaving the house, Dr. Morelle walked briskly down the drive. He hesitated as there was a sudden rustling in the bushes, and Miss Frayle cautiously poked her head out, her hair all awry.

Dr. Morelle stopped, ostensibly to light a cigarette.

'I'm going now to see Mr. Lorrimer — wait for me in the house,' he instructed Miss Frayle tersely. Then he smiled faintly. 'By the way, that was really quite ingenious, that boiler device. You used your brains for once. Quite surprising!'

Having delivered this surprising comment, he threw away the match and walked on.

Miss Frayle gazed after him with a tender smile after this generous and unexpected compliment.

★   ★   ★

Dr. Morelle entered the gardens surrounding Peter Lorrimer's cottage, striding purposely to the front door, where he knocked.

At length Peter Lorrimer opened the door. Dr. Morelle noted with professional interest that the man's face was haggard with worry. He glared at his unwanted visitor.

'Go away, I'm busy. If it's money you want, I haven't got any.'

Dr. Morelle smiled reassuringly. 'The financial implications of the matter I wish to discuss with you are entirely to your advantage. I wish to offer you some employment — in a literary capacity.'

Peter hesitated, then decided to let Dr. Morelle come in. Once he was inside, he closed the door quickly.

Dr. Morelle followed Peter into his living room. The haggard man did not invite him to be seated.

'Well?' he demanded bluntly.

Dr. Morelle assumed a breezy military bearing. 'My name is Welton, Captain Roger Welton. I'm starting a publishing firm in Exeter. I want someone to write a guidebook for me — light amusing stuff, you know. Your name was given to me.'

'Oh?' Peter spoke listlessly.

'You look ill,' Dr. Morelle told him frankly. 'What's the matter with you?'

'Nothing . . . nothing,' Peter muttered. 'I'm all right.'

However, the man certainly didn't look all right. To Dr. Morelle's professional gaze, he was behaving in the manner of a very sick man and his declaration was totally unconvincing.

'You don't *look* all right,' Dr. Morelle pursued. 'Have you seen a doctor?'

'What good are doctors?'

'I should go all the same,' Dr. Morelle told him. 'A doctor or a psychiatrist. Nerve strain can play havoc with the healthiest of men.'

Peter looked at him sharply.

'Who said anything about nerve strain?'

'Perhaps something has gone wrong

with your plot?' Dr. Morelle suggested.

'Plot?'

'Of your latest story, I mean,' Dr. Morelle said smoothly. 'Whatever it is, there is only one cure — relaxation.'

As he spoke, a shaft of sunlight was shining through the window directly on to his face, causing his eyes to gleam and glisten. He unbuttoned his coat, revealing that he had a monocle hanging against his waistcoat on a black silk thread. As he spoke, he held the thread in his fingers so that the monocle began to swing gently to and fro, so that it too winked and glistened in the sunshine.

'That is the secret for over-taxed nerves,' Dr. Morelle murmured. 'Relax! Empty your brain of all thought . . . allow all your resistance to subside . . . as it were anaesthetize your will.'

Peter began to become irritated, and blinked heavily. 'For heaven's sake, don't fiddle with that eyeglass!'

Dr. Morelle dropped the eyeglass and changed his tone. 'I must apologise for sermonising when I really came to see you on business.'

Peter frowned. 'Can't we discuss it some other time?'

'It won't take a minute,' Dr. Morelle said quickly.

Somewhat reluctantly, Peter seated himself at his desk, and Dr. Morelle dropped into a nearby chair.

'Let me tell you about it. It's a pocket guide with a new twist to it . . . '

He picked up his despatch case and unstrapped it while continuing his sales talk:

' . . . we arrange with all the hotel keepers in the district to let us have weekly a list of guests. Then we mail each of them a copy, and that gives us the circulation to attract the advertising on which we live. Of course it has to be well written, just in case anyone starts reading it! Let me show you the sort of make-up we have in mind.'

Dr. Morelle now extracted from his case a small booklet and put the case on the desk. However, in doing so he successfully contrived to knock the large pile of papers on to the floor. With profuse apologies, he leapt up and started to pick the papers up.

'Oh, how very careless of me. Don't move, please! I'll pick them up. I do hope they weren't in any particular order.'

Dr. Morelle's purposefully questing hands picked up the will, which Miss Frayle had found on her visit, together with another paper of similar size, and a document which looked like a Registration Certificate.

Scowling, Peter snatched the papers out of Dr. Morelle's hands and thrust them into a drawer. 'Leave them alone, please. *I'll* pick them up.'

He hurriedly collected the rest of the papers and also put them into a drawer.

'Now, about this little pocket guidebook . . . ' Dr. Morelle began.

'I'm not interested,' Peter snapped.

Dr. Morelle made another attempt. 'Can't I persuade you to change your mind? We propose to develop it into something big, you know. The money may not be large for the first job but — mighty oaks from little acorns grow, what?'

'I'm sorry, I haven't time.'

'Oh, I see. You're already making good

money with your books and short stories. Is that it?'

'Yes,' Peter snapped.

Dr. Morelle rose. 'Lucky man! Young, unencumbered and as one might say, *the sole beneficiary.*'

Peter gave a start. 'What?'

'From the proceeds of your work, of course!' Dr. Morelle said blandly. 'Good day. Don't worry. I'll see myself out.'

Dr. Morelle walked briskly away from the cottage. He had not gone very far, however, before he stopped. Pulling out his notebook he jotted down a few words. He looked at his watch, and moved off down the road.

After a few minutes he came to a telephone box, and went inside.

He inserted coins in the box, and consulted a pencilled list of the calls he proposed to make.

'Messrs. Biddle & Rumble, Solicitors ... Scotland Yard ... all local Registry offices ... ' he muttered to himself, tapping impatiently at the receiver rest. 'Miss Frayle should be doing this detail work!'

* * *

The door to the incinerator in the grounds of Kimber's property opened, letting in a bright shaft of sunlight. A man's figure appeared, unrecognisable when silhouetted against the bright light. Entering quickly, he closed the door behind him.

Darkness closed in, until the man switched on an electric torch, swinging the beam round the shed as the man searched for something. He froze as he heard the noise of the latch of the door being raised behind him. He immediately switched off the torch, and darkness descended again.

The door slowly opened, once more admitting Miss Frayle.

She came into the shed gingerly, leaving the door open, and expecting to find the body of Bensall.

Her eyes widened in horrified surprise when she saw that the body was no longer there. She stood for a moment in indecision, and then started searching for something on the ground.

Further into the shed, the man who had entered earlier stood motionless in the shadow of the oven.

Miss Frayle, her head bent as she continued to search on the ground, slowly came nearer to him. She carried straight on until her head bumped into the stationary figure.

At once she looked up, let out a piercing scream and jumped back, edging back into the sunlight.

She was about to scream again when the man slipped out of the shadows — and revealed himself to be none other than Dr. Morelle.

'Please, Miss Frayle, try and refrain from screaming in that discordant manner.'

Miss Frayle's relief was palpable. 'Oh, what a shock you gave me!'

'You could have avoided it if you'd waited at Barren Tor as I told you,' Dr. Morelle admonished.

'I suppose I shouldn't have come really . . . ' She broke off and again looked round. 'But I suddenly remembered that I'd dropped something.' Failing to find what she was looking for, she looked up at Dr. Morelle, who was watching her performance with controlled impatience.

'But, Dr. Morelle, I don't understand this. Bensall's gone! And he was lying there!'

'His body was removed by the murderer,' Dr. Morelle said calmly. 'That was only to be expected.'

'Then surely we oughtn't to be walking about in here. There may be footprints . . . ' She paused, then added brightly, 'We could take plaster casts.'

'By a regrettable oversight I omitted to fill my pockets with plaster,' Dr. Morelle said dryly. 'And now may I ask what has brought you here? What are you searching for?'

'I suddenly remembered that I'd dropped my handkerchief here last night,' Miss Frayle replied worriedly.

'Your handkerchief?'

'Miss Frayle nodded, 'Yes, I used it for poor Bensall's wound — tried to stop the blood . . . '

'Was it a small one?' Dr. Morelle interrupted sharply. 'Obviously a woman's handkerchief?'

Miss Frayle gave him a puzzled glance. 'Yes. But . . . '

Dr. Morelle frowned. 'You haven't found it?'

Miss Frayle looked about her. 'No. It should have been lying just there.' She pointed to the middle of the floor near the door.

Dr. Morelle gripped her firmly but gently by the arm as he spoke levelly:

'You realize, Miss Frayle, the implication?'

'No!' Miss Frayle looked her puzzlement.

'The absence of the handkerchief,' Dr. Morelle said heavily, 'proves that Bensall's murderer found it when he removed the body.'

'That's Kimber,' Miss Frayle said emphatically. 'He knew about Bensall last night . . . said he'd sent him away . . . it *must* be him!'

'What I'm trying to emphasize to you, Miss Frayle,' Dr. Morelle said patiently, 'is, not the identity of the murderer, but the fact that you are in the greatest personal danger.'

'*I* am?' Miss Frayle asked blankly.

'Now that the murderer knows you were

here at the actual time of the murder, he has only one course open to him.'

'What's that?' Miss Frayle stammered nervously.

'To murder you, Miss Frayle!'

Miss Frayle gave a strangled gasp of terror and turned in a panic, making for the door.

Anticipating her move, Dr. Morelle strode forward quickly and again grabbed her by the arm. She swung to face him, her lips trembling.

'That's why I'm not going to let you out of my sight till I've cleared everything up.'

Miss Frayle calmed, and gave a little shudder.

'I'll accompany you back to the house, via the back entrance. Kimber's penchant for keeping his study curtained will aid us considerably.'

* * *

Miss Frayle paced up and down her bedroom with a distinctly worried expression. In total contrast, Dr. Morelle

76

sprawled lazily in a chair by the fire, apparently at peace with the world. He looked up and regarded her with disdain.

'My dear Miss Frayle, I would be greatly obliged if you would kindly settle somewhere. I find your persistent leaping about the room, like a startled goat, most disturbing.'

'It's all right for you, Dr. Morelle!' Miss Frayle was indignant. 'You're not likely to be murdered any minute.'

Dr. Morelle smiled faintly. 'I always feel a most profound pity for those whose intellectual attainment does not provide a philosophy to cover such a contingency. There is a chance, as you say, that you may be struck down this evening — if my plans for your protection should prove inadequate. Very well, but you take rather similar chances every moment of every day. For all you know, the ceiling above your head may be structurally unsound and fall on you this very instant.'

Instinctively Miss Frayle looked up and ducked involuntarily.

'That nail file,' Dr. Morelle resumed, 'with which you are fidgeting may, at this moment, be depositing some fatal virus in some indiscernible puncture in your epidermis . . . '

Thoroughly alarmed, Miss Frayle hurled the nail file from her, on to the dressing table.

Doctor Morelle continued relentlessly: ' . . . tomorrow, you will have to cross a road . . . '

'Dr. Morelle — please!'

Doctor Morelle regarded her with an air of pained surprise, which was not entirely convincing. 'I am merely endeavouring, my dear Miss Frayle, to give you a comforting philosophy.'

Miss Frayle looked pained. 'If that's your idea of a — ' She broke off abruptly as the telephone rang. 'Kimber!' she exclaimed, glancing at Dr. Morelle in indecision.

'Answer it,' he instructed calmly.

'What are you doing?' Kimber's voice came over the line.

'Oh — Ch-changing, sir,' Miss Frayle faltered.

'Get to the kitchen at once, and get on with supper,' Kimber instructed harshly. 'For two, Mr. Lorrimer's coming.'

'V-very good, sir.'

Dr. Morelle, who had been able to overhear Kimber's barked instructions, smiled complacently.

'And,' Kimber added, 'I want the sherry and two glasses put in the study.'

'Yes, sir.'

As Miss Frayle hung up, Dr. Morelle jumped up from his chair. 'And now to work!'

Going over to the door, he very quietly unlocked it. Then he opened it gingerly and looked out into the corridor. On seeing that the coast was clear, he turned to Miss Frayle.

'Directly I'm outside, lock the door again.'

'But, Dr. Morelle . . . '

'Lock the door and stay here till I send for you. Do as I say.'

He slipped out into the passage, closing the door behind him.

Miss Frayle hesitated for a moment, and then locked the door as she had been instructed.

★   ★   ★

Seen from the outside, Kimber's mansion was in darkness, except for a light in the hall, which threw a dim glow over the drive before the front door.

Peter Lorrimer stood for a moment surveying the house, then he moved towards the back of it.

★ ★ ★

In her bedroom, Miss Frayle wandered over to the mantelpiece. Evidently still restless, she looked at the clock. Her lips tightened as she came to a decision. Turning, she went over to the door and unlocked it.

She opened it just a few inches and listened. All was quiet.

Making up her mind not to wait any longer, she pulled the door wide enough to slip out, putting her hand to the light switch.

Miss Frayle tiptoed along the corridor towards the stairs. She paused and listened. All was still quiet. The light was on in the hall. Slowly she started to go down the stairs.

Miss Frayle was halfway down the stairs when there suddenly sounded a loud and eerie screeching wail. She was so startled she nearly fell, but managed to save herself by clutching at the banister.

As the eerie wail was repeated, she looked about her desperately, but saw nothing to account for the sound.

Heaving a sigh of relief she continued down the stairs. Reaching Kimber's study, she listened outside for a moment, but heard nothing. She was just straightening when she was grabbed from behind, and a hand clamped brutally over her mouth.

★   ★   ★

Kimber propelled himself into the hall in his wheelchair. Closing the front door, he proceeded to enter his study.

The only light in the curtained room came from the desk lamp, and seated at the desk, calmly smoking, was Dr. Morelle.

Kimber stared in disbelief. 'What the

hell — !' he exploded.

'Come in, Mr. Kimber,' Dr. Morelle said pleasantly, 'come in.'

Kimber propelled his wheelchair up to the desk. Judging by his angry expression, he was working himself up into one of his towering rages.

'Relax, Mr. Kimber,' Dr. Morelle said calmly. 'I've been waiting for a chat with you.'

Kimber flushed angrily. 'May I ask, Professor Harper . . . '

'No, Mr. Kimber,' Dr. Morelle interrupted blandly. 'That was, I'm ashamed to say, somewhat wide of the truth. Actually, my name is Morelle, Dr. Morelle.'

He paused, awaiting a reaction from Kimber, who only frowned in bewilderment.

'Dr. Morelle?'

'D'you mean to say that name doesn't mean anything to you?'

'Nothing at all!' Kimber snapped. 'Now, will you kindly explain to me how you got into my house, and what you think you're doing here!'

'I told you, I wanted a further chat with you.'

Kimber narrowed his eyes. 'What about?'

'The murder of your stepdaughter, Mr. Kimber!'

The unexpectedness of this verbal attack appeared to take the wind out of Kimber's sails. He slumped in his chair, staring open-mouthed at his visitor.

Dr. Morelle leaned forward so that the light of the desk lamp shone directly on his face. At the same time he started to swing his eyeglass to and fro so that it kept catching and reflecting the light.

'A matter on which I think you can throw a great deal of light.'

Kimber licked his lips and tried to pull himself together. But his eyes kept following the swing of the flashing eyeglass.

'I don't know what you're talking about. Who led you to believe my stepdaughter was murdered?'

Dr. Morelle kept staring intently at Kimber, and steadily swinging his eyeglass, which consistently riveted Kimber's gaze.

'You did, Mr. Kimber.'

'Nonsense. She's just — gone away.'

'Where to?' Dr. Morelle asked sharply.

'I don't know. And anyway, it's no business of yours.'

'Possibly she went away — with Bensall. He's away too, isn't he?'

Kimber squirmed in his chair, but his eyes were still held by the swinging eyeglass.

'You'd prefer her to be with Bensall rather than — Peter Lorrimer?' Dr. Morelle suggested.

'Why should I mind if she were with Peter Lorrimer?'

'Because he'd insist on your paying over her inheritance, Mr. Kimber.'

Kimber made one final effort to regain control of the situation. Straightening up, he shouted: 'Why should I answer your questions. Get out of my house. Get out — !'

Dr. Morelle leaned over the desk, catching Kimber by his shoulder, and forcing him back into his chair.

'Sit back, Mr. Kimber, and relax!'

From where Kimber sat, he could see Dr. Morelle's eyes flashing in the light, while the eyeglass seemed to glisten more brightly every time it swung back and forth . . . back and forth . . .

'That was what you said to me, wasn't it? Relax, you said . . . surrender your will you said. And now it's the other way round, Mr. Kimber, and I'm going to succeed where you failed . . . '

Kimber was now making a terrific effort to resist Dr. Morelle's hypnosis. But he could not control his eyes, nor indeed now his whole head, which were moving to and fro in time to the swinging eyeglass.

' . . . Because, you see,' Dr. Morelle murmured, 'I happen to be a professional in hypnotism, while you are only an amateur.'

Suddenly Kimber's resistance collapsed. His eyes became fixed and glassy, and he slumped back in his chair.

Dr. Morelle rose from behind the desk he had been leaning across, and came round to look at Kimber. He flipped his fingers under his eyes and grunted with satisfaction when they did not blink. Turning to the windows he called out:

'All right, Inspector!'

From behind the heavy curtains that hid the windows stepped a police Inspector accompanied by his Detective-Sergeant. Both men were in plain clothes.

They came forward and wonderingly looked at Kimber, who continued to sit slumped in his chair, staring straight before him.

Inspector Harris glanced at Dr. Morelle. 'He's really in a hypnotic trance?'

'Try and wake him up,' Dr. Morelle invited, dryly.

Inspector Harris shook Kimber vigorously. 'Mr. Kimber! Mr. Kimber!'

But Kimber did not come round, remained unmoving, staring before him.

The Inspector turned back to Dr. Morelle. 'You've put him under all right. But how's that going to help us?'

'He'll answer any questions I ask him — and truthfully.'

Harris frowned. 'I doubt if we can use any statements made while he's in this condition.'

'I'm not suggesting you should,' Dr. Morelle said smoothly. 'But when he has

86

told us the true story — I emphasise, his *true* story, as he believes it, then I'll waken him, and you can caution him and question him in the ordinary way.'

As Inspector Harris still looked doubtful, Dr. Morelle added: 'Frankly, Inspector, I'm not interested in the legal aspect of this case. All I am concerned with is arriving at the truth. How you deal with the truth when you've heard it is entirely your affair.'

The Inspector nodded. 'Very good, Dr. Morelle. Carry on in your own way.'

Dr. Morelle once more sat down in the chair under the lamp. Gently but firmly he addressed Kimber directly.

'Mr. Kimber, can you hear me?'

'Yes.' Kimber's voice was toneless.

'You will answer my questions with absolute truthfulness?'

'Yes . . . '

*   *   *

The outer door of the hut containing the incinerator was closed, but the place was lit by the glow of the fire coming from the open oven doors. A man was standing by them, feeding the fire with lumps of peat and logs of wood.

The man straightened up and turned, looking across the room to where Miss Frayle was lying against the wall. Her hands were tied behind her back, and a handkerchief was tied across her mouth, acting as an effective gag.

Her eyes revealed that she was in an extremity of terror, as she watched Peter Lorrimer stoking the fire . . .

★ ★ ★

In Kimber's study, watched by the two policemen, Dr. Morelle began his interrogation.

'Why did you keep your stepdaughter virtually a prisoner in this house? Was it so that she would have no opportunity of getting married?'

'Yes,' Kimber assented tonelessly.

'Why did you oppose her marriage? Was it because in that event all the money passed to her under her mother's will?'

'Yes.'

'When she told you she wished to marry Peter Lorrimer, what action did you take?' Dr. Morelle asked shrewdly.

Kimber's eyes were glazed and expressionless, and his voice gentle and matter-of-fact as he answered:

'I decided she must die.'

'How did you plan to kill her?'

'I hypnotised Peter Lorrimer, and when he was under my influence ordered him to kill her, and destroy the remains in the incinerator.'

'And then?' Dr. Morelle prompted.

'After a suitable time, I planned to pass over sufficient evidence to the police for Lorrimer to be convicted of her murder.'

'And Bensall?'

'He was getting suspicious.'

'And the housemaid — Amy? Have you any plans for her?'

'Lorrimer is dealing with her now,' Kimber said emotionlessly.

At this chilling revelation Inspector Harris stepped forward anxiously, but Dr. Morelle waved him back. 'Don't worry,' he reassured him. 'I have taken the necessary precautions. My assistant, Miss

Frayle, alias Amy, is locked in her room, waiting to be sent for.'

Inspector Harris was still concerned. 'But what I don't understand is, surely Lorrimer must realise . . . '

Dr. Morelle shook his head. 'It is a proven fact, Inspector, that the victim of an hypnotic trance has no memory of anything that occurred during that trance.' He glanced at his watch. 'Lorrimer should be here any moment now. I suggest that while we're waiting for him, I get Miss Frayle down, so that when I recall Kimber from his trance, all the principals that remain will be present.'

'Very well.'

'Perhaps Detective-Sergeant Jackson wouldn't mind fetching her?' Dr. Morelle suggested.

'Certainly, sir,' Jackson assented. 'Which room is she in?'

'Right at the top of the house — through the loft.'

'Very good, sir.' Jackson turned to go.

'Should she seem reluctant to unlock the door,' Dr. Morelle added pompously, 'just assure her that it is *I* who have sent for her.'

'Yes, sir,'

As Jackson left the room, Dr. Morelle turned to the Inspector. 'Miss Frayle has a genius for doing the right thing at the wrong moment — which is only exceeded by her capacity for doing the wrong thing at the right moment.'

'Er — quite.' The Inspector looked nonplussed for a moment, then moved on to a point that had been puzzling him. 'Tell me, Dr. Morelle, what put you on to Kimber's hypnotism stunt?'

Dr. Morelle smiled thinly. 'The poor deluded man actually had the effrontery to try his skill on me! Then I took a glance at those books' — he waved a hand to the wall bookshelves — 'practically every book that's ever been written on the subject of hypnotism is on those shelves. I at once realized that the man was a self-taught amateur.'

At that moment he door opened and Jackson came hurrying back — alone.

'Excuse me, sir, but there's no one in that room.'

For once, Dr. Morelle was completely nonplussed. 'No one there?' he said slowly.

'The door isn't locked either,' Jackson went on. 'I looked in. The room's empty.'

Dr. Morelle realized what had happened. Frowning, he said: 'As usual, she must have disobeyed instructions. The crass little idiot! And with Lorrimer about!'

He raced across the room to the door, calling to the two policemen as he went: 'Come along, both of you!'

Inspector Harris hesitated, pointing to Kimber. 'But what about him?'

Dr. Morelle looked back at him from the doorway. 'He won't move till I release him. Now come along with me!'

The two men followed him out of the study. 'There's the kitchen, Inspector.' Dr. Morelle pointed to it across the hall. 'Have a look in there, will you?'

The Inspector hurried to the kitchen door while Dr. Morelle, followed by Jackson, rushed up the stairs. Reaching the top, they hurried along the corridor to the door of Miss Frayle's room.

Dr. Morelle flung open the door and switched on the light. Striding into it he saw that the room was indeed empty. Meanwhile Jackson was examining the lock.

'Key's on the inside, sir. There's no sign of the lock being tampered with.'

For once in his life, Dr. Morelle was really perturbed. When he spoke, his somewhat pompous manner had temporarily vanished.

'It's as I feared. That girl's sheer bone from the neck up!' Noticing that the curtains were not drawn, he crossed to the window and examined it rapidly to see if anyone could have climbed in. The window was firmly closed. He looked back at Jackson as he stood by the door. 'Let's get back downstairs.'

Jackson switched off the light and went out. Dr. Morelle strode across the darkened room to join him, then paused as, out of the corner of his eye, he noticed a flickering red glow reflected in the dressing table mirror.

Quickly he spun round and hurried to the window and looked out. Above the trees at one point was a dull red glow, getting brighter. As he looked a thick spiral of smoke rose up.

'My God! That's the incinerator!' Turning, he plunged after Jackson.

'Quick! Find the Inspector — make for the back door! We've got to get to the incinerator outside. There's just a chance — if we hurry!'

* * *

Peter Lorrimer turned back to the fire and checked that it was burning fiercely. Then he crossed to the bound figure of Miss Frayle, who shrank away against the wall.

Getting hold of her, he jerked her up and dragged her across the room towards the fire.

Miss Frayle struggled frantically, inarticulate sounds issuing from her gag.

With a snarl of rage, Lorrimer suddenly extended his hands around her throat and started to strangle her.

Then the door of the shed was kicked open from the outside, and Dr. Morelle, followed by the Inspector and Jackson, came rushing in.

Peter Lorrimer dropped his hands from Miss Frayle's throat and dived for the door.

Expertly the two police officers caught hold of him, and after a short sharp struggle, brought him under control.

Meanwhile Dr. Morelle was attending to Miss Frayle.

Quickly he untied her hands and removed the handkerchief gag. Miss Frayle lay limply against him with her eyes closed. Very tenderly, he looked at the imprints of Lorrimer's fingers on her neck. Very gently, he began to massage her throat.

'That's very nice!' Miss Frayle murmured, her eyes still closed.

'Miss Frayle!'

At Dr. Morelle's sharp exclamation, Miss Frayle opened her eyes and smiled lovingly at him.

'I knew you'd get here in time!'

Dr. Morelle gave her a severe look. 'May I point out that if only you'd obeyed my instructions, it wouldn't have been necessary to come here at all!'

He helped her to her feet, where she swayed unsteadily in his arms.

Nearby Peter Lorrimer was being firmly held by Inspector Harris and Jackson. He was staring straight in front of him with glazed and staring eyes. Suddenly he shivered violently, blinked his eyes rapidly and looked around him with a puzzled, vacant expression.

'Where am I?' he muttered. 'What's happening?' He stared at his captors. 'Who are you?'

After making sure that Miss Frayle was sufficiently recovered to stand on her feet, Dr. Morelle crossed over to Peter Lorrimer.

'You don't remember me, Mr. Lorrimer?

'No.' Lorrimer appeared bewildered, then: 'Yes! You're Captain Welton.'

Dr. Morelle smiled faintly. 'No longer, I'm afraid. I have abandoned the publishing business in favour of detection.'

'Detecting what?'

'A murderer, Mr. Lorrimer.'

Lorrimer looked at him in confusion.

'But, I don't understand.'

'You soon will,' Dr. Morelle said implacably. He turned to Inspector Harris. 'And now I suggest we return to Barren Tor, so that we can settle matters with Mr. Kimber as well.'

* * *

In his study, Kimber was still lying back in his wheelchair, staring ahead with fixed unblinking eyes. Dr. Morelle was seated at the desk opposite him as before, but now Miss Frayle, with Peter Lorrimer between the Inspector and Jackson, were seated round in a rough semi-circle.

'And now,' Dr. Morelle resumed, 'I think we can deal with the final phase of this somewhat unusual case.' He leaned forward, and passed his fingers two or three times across Kimber's eyes. He spoke in a low voice:

'Mr. Kimber. This is Dr. Morelle speaking. Wake up, Mr. Kimber!'

Kimber shivered violently, blinking his eyes rapidly several times. Suddenly he sat up and looked around him with a

97

bewildered expression, which rapidly turned into one of anger.

'What's happening here?' he demanded.' His puzzled gaze settled on the two policemen, before swinging back to Dr. Morelle. 'Who are these two men?'

'These are Inspector Harris and Detective-Sergeant Jackson of the County Police.'

Kimber visibly flinched. 'Police!'

'Mr. Lorrimer you know,' Dr. Morelle resumed. 'Also Amy . . . '

As Kimber took in the presence of Peter Lorrimer and Miss Frayle, he betrayed a quick flash of alarm.

' . . . alias my personal assistant, Miss Frayle.'

Apparently realizing that he was in a tight corner, Kimber tried to bluster.

'Get out of my house, all of you! Get out this moment!'

'You're being a little hasty, Mr. Kimber,' Dr. Morelle said. 'These gentlemen are anxious to have a few words with you,'

'I've got nothing to say to them,' Kimber snapped.

Dr. Morelle smiled grimly. 'Perhaps

you will have, when I tell you that you have already given them the full details of your dastardly plot.'

'I've given them details?' Kimber was clearly shaken. 'Of my plot?'

'Certainly — while in an hypnotic trance which I induced,' Dr. Morelle said smugly. 'Rather a case of the biter bit, isn't it, Mr. Kimber?'

Kimber was now thoroughly frightened. 'You hypnotized me?'

Dr. Morelle nodded grimly. 'What you said in the trance may not be filed in evidence against you. But Miss Frayle here is a material witness. She will identify the charred bones in the incinerator as those of your stepdaughter by means of this earring . . .' He paused as he picked up a sapphire earring from the desk, holding it before him. '. . . which was found by her a moment or two before Bensall was murdered. So if you will take my advice, Mr. Kimber, you will do well to make a free and frank confession of how you plotted to get rid of your stepdaughter by hypnotising Peter Lorrimer, and using him to murder for you by proxy.'

Before Kimber could make any response to the damning accusation, Peter Lorrimer leapt to his feet. His face blazing with anger, he rushed at Kimber, and caught him by the throat.

He began shaking Kimber to and fro like a dog with a rat.

'You swine! You devil! You made me kill her — and I never knew! You made me kill Cynthia, whom I loved, whom I was going to marry. You devil, I'll kill you for it!'

Recovering from their surprise, the Inspector and Jackson jumped forward. Getting hold of Peter Lorrimer, they managed to drag him away from Kimber, who was now cowering in his chair, all resistance gone.

'So you see,' Dr. Morelle resumed, 'what was coming to you, Mr. Kimber — if your plot had succeeded.'

The others looked their puzzlement.

'But it did succeed!' Inspector Harris exclaimed.

Dr. Morelle shook his head, smiling thinly: 'On the contrary. You see, he *thought* he had hypnotized this young man, but in actual fact he *hadn't*!'

'What are you talking about?' Lorrimer demanded.

'Peter Lorrimer,' Dr. Morelle explained complacently, 'is resistant to any hypnotic influence. I tested him myself when I called on him in my capacity of Captain Welton. But when Mr. Kimber decided to test his amateur capabilities on him, with commendable initiative Peter Lorrimer seized on this golden opportunity.'

Miss Frayle showed a sudden flash of insight. 'You mean, he only *pretended* to be hypnotised, but wasn't?'

'Precisely, my dear Miss Frayle. And quite apart from his natural immunity to hypnotism, had Mr. Lorrimer really loved Cynthia, it is very doubtful that he could have been hypnotized to kill her. Kimber, as an amateur, probably wasn't aware of that.'

Peter Lorrimer's eyes blazed with anger. 'You must be mad! Why in heaven's name should I want to kill the girl I was going to marry!'

'Because . . . ' Dr. Morelle picked up

some notes, which were lying before him on the desk, ' . . . because, firstly, you knew it would be a bigamous marriage, seeing that you were married in Birmingham on the 14th of April last to a Miss Lucy Adams, who is alive today.'

Lorrimer remained silent, staring at Dr. Morelle with baleful intensity.

'And secondly,' Dr. Morelle resumed, 'because in the desk in your cottage lies Cynthia Mason's will, leaving everything to you.'

Dr. Morelle paused, and looked at Miss Frayle, smiling sardonically. 'I heard all about Cynthia's *mother's* will from Miss Frayle . . . who, with her well-known capacity for searching for haystacks in needles, naturally missed the one document which elucidated the whole matter.'

Miss Frayle blushed and squirmed in her seat, both indignant and ashamed of hearing her efforts thus described.

Following Dr. Morelle's revelations, everyone in the room was looking at Peter Lorrimer, except Kimber, who was hunched up in his chair with his face in his hands.

'Cynthia Mason was murdered deliberately and cold-bloodedly by Peter Lorrimer,' Dr. Morelle went on implacably. 'He did not, however, kill Bensall. That was Mr. Kimber's work.'

Kimber looked up at this. 'It's not true — I deny it!' he said shrilly. 'How could I? I'm a cripple — I can't get down to the incinerator shed.'

Inspector Harris, who had been following the revelations with a furrowed brow, shot a glance at Dr. Morelle. 'Doctor — ?'

'Kindly note the first piece of evidence, Inspector. Mr. Kimber knew that Bensall had been killed in the incinerator shed. A fact known only to Miss Frayle, you, me and the murderer.'

'It's nonsense,' Kimber protested, 'all this — lying nonsense . . .'

'Now for the second piece of evidence,' Dr. Morelle said complacently. He reached into a drawer of Kimber's desk, and extracted from it a bloodstained handkerchief.

'Miss Frayle's handkerchief, with which she tried to staunch Bensall's wound, and which you found when you went to recover the body. I saw it in your drawer on the occasion when you so kindly went to assist Miss Frayle with the kitchen boiler.'

'It's preposterous, what you're saying.' Kimber remained defiant. 'The handkerchief is mine — I cut my hand . . . '

Dr. Morelle's voice cut like a lash. 'It is now you who is talking nonsense, Mr. Kimber. A third piece of evidence — a rather sensational piece . . . '

He took from his pocket a small photograph, which he held up with its reverse side to Kimber.

' . . . a photograph of *you*, Mr. Kimber, in the act of murdering Bensall!'

With a strangled cry, Kimber jumped to his feet from the wheelchair and ran to Dr. Morelle to snatch the photograph from him.

Dr. Morelle calmly turned the face of the photograph so that Kimber could now see it for what it really was — a snapshot of a small child.

Kimber immediately halted, suddenly realizing that he had given away the fact that he could walk.

'A rather dubious little ruse, but it appears to have worked,' Dr. Morelle commented dryly, returning the photograph to his pocket. 'The photograph is, in point of fact, of a small niece of mine — but my little deception has established that Mr. Kimber's footwork is as nimble as yours and mine.

'The purpose of his pretence to be crippled was, of course, in the first place, to play on his stepdaughter's sympathies, so that she would be less likely to contemplate leaving him.'

Kimber, realizing that the game was up, sank back again into his wheelchair.

'I think, Inspector,' Dr. Morelle said, 'there is little doubt that we now have sufficient evidence to take Mr. Kimber and Mr. Lorrimer to the gallows.'

Their attention lately having been given entirely to Kimber and Dr. Morelle, both the Inspector and Jackson had unwittingly relaxed their grip on Peter Lorrimer.

Suddenly he threw off their detaining hands and rushed for the door and out into the hall.

Inspector Harris reacted belatedly. 'After him! Quick!'

He rushed out after Lorrimer, followed by Dr. Morelle and Miss Frayle. Jackson stayed behind to guard the scowling Kimber.

Peter Lorrimer was making for the front door when he saw a uniformed policeman standing before it, fully alert and ready to block his exit.

Instead he veered off and rushed up the stairs, to be hotly pursued by Inspector Harris and the policeman.

Dr. Morelle, however, continued to make straight for the front door, dutifully followed by Miss Frayle.

Outside the house a light now came on in an upstairs window. The window was then thrown open, and a body appeared to dive out of it headfirst into the night.

There was a dull, crunching thud as Lorrimer's body hit the drive, the actual impact invisible in the darkness.

Dr. Morelle hurried forward, and far above him, Inspector Harris became silhouetted in the window.

Sick with horror, Miss Frayle turned

away, leaning against the front door frame, breathing hard.

She turned as Dr. Morelle moved back to her. 'Is he . . . ?' She was unable to complete her whispered sentence.

'Killed instantaneously,' Dr. Morelle said gently. 'Perhaps it's the best way out.'

As Miss Frayle began shivering violently, Dr. Morelle put his arm round her shoulders. She turned to him and gazed into his face . . .

★   ★   ★

In Dr. Morelle's Harley Street study, Dr. Morelle was still dictating his account of the affair of the missing heiress, and Miss Frayle was busily taking it down in shorthand.

'And as I gazed deep into Miss Frayle's strained white face . . . '

Miss Frayle's pencil stopped. She gazed lovingly at Dr Morelle, a tremulous smile upon her lips.

' . . . I breathed a silent prayer of gratitude to my creator that he had endowed me with sufficient common-sense to remain a bachelor.'

Dr. Morelle leaned back and gazed blandly at the ceiling, blowing smoke rings.

Miss Frayle's tremulous smile changed to an expression of disgruntled disappointment — and there came the sound of a sharp click as she jabbed viciously at her notebook — and again broke the point of her pencil.

2

The Case of the Queenpin

Doctor Morelle has visited the majority of the countries of the globe. He has lectured in New York and Paris, Capetown and Ottawa, Belgrade and Auckland. But in recent years he has rarely moved from London. He says that, in spite of all the losses resulting from the war, the library facilities of London — as necessary for the abstruse researches in which he is so often concerned — are as good as anywhere in the world. And his house in Harley Street has for him become more of a home than any other residence which he has occupied in the past twenty years or so.

As a result he usually shows a marked reluctance to leave London for medical purposes, and he has been known to turn down an offer to undertake a consultation in some distant city, even when the fee offered is considerable, merely because he does not wish to spend any length of time away from Britain's capital.

It was, however, both the offer of a tempting fee, and the fact that the offer came from an old friend and colleague whom he did not like to 'let down', that made him travel to the old city of Kingston-upon-Hull (commonly known as Hull) in order to take part in a joint consultation concerning a young man afflicted with the distressing mental condition known as paranoia.

The case did not prove as complex as as he had feared, and Doctor Morelle and his medical friend, now installed in a comfortable practice in Hull, were soon able to come to an agreement as to the best course of treatment to be pursued. When this stage had been reached, Doctor Morelle returned to the pleasant hotel where he had taken the precaution of booking rooms. In the lounge he found Miss Frayle waiting for him. It was fairly late in the evening, and she seemed to be more than a trifle anxious. Though the Doctor was unable to see the reason for her anxiety.

'Oh, there you are, Doctor Morelle,' she said in somewhat relieved tones as he entered the hotel lounge. 'I was just beginning to wonder whatever had happened to you.'

'Pyschological consultations are frequently of considerable duration, Miss Frayle,' he replied in an irritated manner, and then relaxing a little, he went on: 'I trust, however, that you have been able to occupy your evening in a profitable manner.'

Miss Frayle smiled. 'Oh, yes, Doctor,' she said. 'I've been to the pictures. It was a lovely film, all about the life of a young doctor. He was so attractive and charming.' She paused and sighed deeply. 'The film was nothing at all like real life, of course.'

Doctor Morelle found a certain source of irritation in Miss Frayle's romantic outlook on life, and the present was, he thought, one of the most unpleasing of such occasions.

'I regret,' he said, 'that members of the medical profession in some strange manner known only to themselves fail to conform to your sentimental imaginings.'

Miss Frayle sighed again. 'Oh, well,' she said, 'I suppose that you can't have everything in this life.'

She looked around her carefully, as if she wanted to be sure that no one was sufficiently near to overhear what she was saying. Indeed, the only other occupant of the lounge — an elderly gentleman with a red face — was clearly buried in his copy of *The Times*, which he was reading with such care and attention that it was clear enough that he would not be bothered to listen to any conversation which might be taking place. And he now left them.

Miss Frayle grasped the Doctor's arm convulsively. 'Doctor,' she murmured in dramatic tones, 'there's something queer going on in this hotel.'

The Doctor looked even more irritated than was his wont. Lack of precision on the part of anyone to whom he was talking was always one of the things which most annoyed him.

'What precisely does that exceedingly

vague remark imply, Miss Frayle?' he demanded.

Miss Frayle looked somewhat taken aback by this demand to make any sort of precise formulation of what it was that had struck her as being queer about the hotel, but she knew that she would have to give the Doctor some justification for what she had said.

'Well, while I've been waiting here for you,' she remarked, 'people have been bustling in and out, and the Manager looks simply worried to death. Then — I'm sure that there's something very peculiar going on — a man popped into this lounge just now, and, before he went out again in a hurry — he gave me the strangest look.'

Doctor Morelle looked completely nonplussed by this recital of what Miss Fayle regarded as the facts of the case.

'You amaze me, Miss Frayle!' he exclaimed. 'Ah, I am afraid that your ever-fervid imagination has been somewhat over-stimulated by the cinematic exhibition which you have been witnessing during my absence in the hospital.'

Miss Frayle was not convinced by this apparently reasonable explanation of the matters that had been exciting her during the Doctor's absence.

'But, Doctor, I tell you,' she began to expostulate, and then broke off. 'Look!' she exclaimed, 'there's the man now — the man I was talking about. He's just coming in again. And the Manager is with him.'

'Good evening, Doctor Morelle,' said the newcomer, holding out his hand and smiling in a friendly manner. 'I'm Detective-Inspector Grant. I thought that I recognized your Miss Frayle when I was in here earlier on.'

Miss Frayle giggled helplessly. 'Oh, is that why you stared so hard at me,' she said.

The Inspector laughed. 'Yes, that's right, Miss Frayle,' he said. 'Sorry if it worried you. But that's what becomes of being famous, you see.'

Doctor Morelle frowned portentously, and the Inspector caught a glimpse of his expression, adding quickly: 'And, of course, being assistant to someone famous too.'

Doctor Morelle seemed to be getting impatient at the course of this conversation.

'I presume,' he said, 'that your object in honouring us with this unexpected visit is not entirely due to your desire to pay us compliments.'

The Inspector appeared a little surprised at this sudden wordy onslaught.

'Indeed, no, Doctor,' he said hastily, 'though, naturally, it's pleasant to meet people so well known as Miss Frayle and yourself. But the moment the Manager here told me that you were staying in his hotel, I knew that you were the one man who would be able to help me in the little job which is on my plate tonight.'

'I knew that something queer was going on here,' announced Miss Frayle in tones of triumph, utter and unconcealed. 'What exactly has been happening?'

'It's nothing much, really,' the Manager hastily explained. 'But if it gets at all generally known in the neighbourhood, it's sure that it won't do my hotel any good.'

Inspector Grant grinned. 'Nonsense!'

he said. 'Whatever happens, nobody's going to blame *you* for it. What's happened is in no way your fault, after all.'

'I'm not so sure,' the Manager replied. 'You know how people talk in a place like this.'

Doctor Morelle was getting more and more impatient and annoyed at the way in which things were developing.

'Perhaps,' he said, 'Inspector Grant would be so kind as to divulge to me the cause of your apprehension. After all, your cryptic utterances are completely meaningless to me, and I should like to be enlightened a little — that is, Inspector, if the whole affair is not of too confidential a nature to be divulged to anyone outside the immediate circle of those concerned.'

The Inspector at once became very apologetic.

'I'm very sorry, Doctor, to have rattled on like that without giving you any explanation,' he said. 'As a matter of fact, I was just going to tell you all about it. Between you and me — and Miss Frayle of course! — we've run a notorious fence to earth. She's been staying in this hotel. Name of Carla Donetti. She is, in effect, the kingpin of an organised bunch of crooks who we've been after for a long time.'

Miss Frayle giggled impulsively. 'Surely you mean the queenpin, Inspector,' she corrected him.

'That's right, Miss,' he said with a laugh. 'As a matter of fact, they've been blowing round the country knocking off a lot of very valuable pictures — old masters and all that. They've been cutting them out of the frames, and then disposing of them to unscrupulous collectors on the continent.'

The Manager added seriously: 'To look at her,' he said, 'she is the last sort of person that you'd expect to be engaged in that sort of business, you know. Always dressed in the absolute height of fashion — smart, elegant . . . '

'On the contrary,' Doctor Morelle interrupted him, 'your description at once suggests to me the type of individual who might well be expected to be engaging herself in nefarious practices of all kinds.'

'The Doctor,' Miss Frayle patiently explained, 'does not altogether approve of smart, elegant women, Mr. Denham.'

Doctor Morelle cast a meaningful glance at Miss Frayle. 'No doubt our friend the Manager will have observed that for himself,' he retorted.

While Miss Frayle was endeavouring to extract the meaning of this venomous thrust, the Doctor was resuming his conversation with Inspector Grant.

'You were saying, Inspector,' he went on to ask, 'that you have trapped the woman at this hotel?'

The Inspector rubbed his nose ruefully with the back of his hand.

'That's just what we haven't done, I'm afraid, Doctor,' he said. 'She's managed to give us the slip, just when we were ready to close the net and get hold of the whole gang of crooks. Most unfortunate bit of timing.'

'Oh, dear!' Miss Frayle murmured, feeling entirely sympathetic with the Inspector in his plight.

The Inspector, however, resumed a

little more cheerfully: 'But I've picked up her maid, who had also been staying here. Of course, it doesn't necessarily follow that she's in any way implicated in the crimes, but I'm just going to ask her a few questions. I'd be very glad if you'd stay here and give me any helpful tips as to what she has to say, Doctor.'

Mr. Denham, the Manager, now said: 'Here's your Sergeant now, Inspector, with the girl.'

'Oh, yes.' Inspector Grant replied. 'Thank you, Sergeant. Come and sit down, Miss,' he added to the girl who was glancing around her in an alarmed fashion. 'There's no need to be frightened. All I want is to know what you know of a Miss Donetti. Oh, Mr. Denham,' he said, turning to the Manager.

'Yes, Inspector?'

'There's no need for us to detain you here any longer. I'm sure that you're a very busy man, and won't have a lot of time to spare over this business. I'll keep you well posted as to what happens from now on.'

'Thanks,' said the Manager, seeing that this amounted to his dismissal from the scene.

'Now,' said the Inspector, when the Manager had left the room, 'let's have your name again.'

'My name's Molly O'Brien,' the girl said, with a very definite trace of Irish brogue in her speech. 'And I'm only over here from Ireland this six months.'

Doctor Morelle looked interested. 'What part of Ireland do you come from?' he asked.

Molly O'Brien looked gently surprised at this question. She was an attractive girl with dark curly hair, and her early frightened expression now seemed to have left her face. Clearly she realized that the best that she could do was to tell the truth.

'I come from Ballymoney, in the North of Ireland, sir,' she said. 'I got my job with Miss Donetti from an employment agency in Liverpool, and since then — during the past six months, as I said — I've been travelling about with her all over the country.'

'What sort of places did you go to with Miss Donetti, Molly?' asked the Inspector.

'Oh, all over the place,' she explained. 'Plymouth, Bristol, Swansea, Cardiff, Portsmouth . . . '

'And you enjoyed your job?' the Inspector asked.

Molly smiled. And her smile was a pleasant sight to see.

'Sure,' she said, 'Miss Donetti is a grand person. We have always stayed at the best hotels, wherever we went. Mind you, I don't know the first thing about her business. She hardly encouraged me to ask any questions about her personal affairs, and so I didn't.'

'I see,' said the Inspector. This, as he had said to Doctor Morelle a few minutes earlier, was just what he had expected. 'And now let's get round to this afternoon. Tell me just what happened, will you? She went out directly after tea, and, as you know, she hasn't come back yet.'

'She did so,' said Molly, with the emphasis on the last word of the sentence.

Miss Frayle's forehead puckered up in surprise, and bewilderment at this response on Molly's part.

'You mean she did go out, but didn't come back?' Miss Frayle asked.

'She did so,' Molly repeated.

The Inspector grinned cheerfully. 'I think I know what she means all right, Miss Frayle,' he said. 'Now, Molly, when she went out, did she take anything with her?'

'I packed a small suitcase for her,' Molly said, 'and that's about all. She gave me a fair amount of money, and said that maybe I'd not be seeing her again for about two weeks. I was to stay on here, she told me, until I heard from her. But that wouldn't be for some time.'

The Inspector looked a little perturbed at this information. It was more or less what he had anticipated, but it was annoying to think that his quarry had escaped him with such a small margin of time and yet so completely.

Doctor Morelle apparently was in no way worried at what had happened, though he clearly considered that there was no more information to obtained from Molly.

'Did she receive any visitors at these various hotels where she stayed?' he asked.

'She did,' Molly said with a smile which suggested infinite possibilities. 'Sometimes two or three of them in one place. They were nearly all men. I often thought to meself that Miss Donetti was a bit of a flighty one.'

Doctor Morelle looked annoyed and irritated. 'I'm not asking you for your impressions,' he snapped. 'Kindly keep to the facts that you know for certain.'

Molly looked a trifle sulky at this rebuke. 'Sure,' she said, 'a girl has a right to her own thoughts without having her head bitten off when she . . . '

Doctor Morelle interrupted her ruthlessly. 'Were there any visitors coming to see her during her stay at *this* hotel?' he asked with considerable emphasis.

'There were not,' Molly replied, her lips still pursed up sulkily. 'Faith, we'd only been here two days, so we had, and I suppose that Miss Donetti had scarcely had time to get to know any of the folk here.'

The door of the lounge swung open suddenly, and the Manager rushed in, his face contorted with excitement.

'Inspector! Doctor Morelle!' he exclaimed in tones that were almost triumphant with delight and excitement.

'What's biting you now, Mr. Denham?' asked Inspector Grant. The Inspector, in. fact, was more than a little annoyed at this interruption, for he had thought that the cross-examination of Molly O'Brien was just showing signs of yielding results of some promise.

'A man has just called at the hotel,' Mr. Denham explained.

'And what about it?'

'He's asked for Miss Donetti,' the Manager said, still very excited in manner.

'Where is he?' exclaimed the Inspector, realizing the vast importance of this news. 'You didn't let him go, did you? You managed to keep him here somehow? This may be the very thing to lead us to Donetti.'

The Manager smiled, with confidence in his own commonsense and good judgment.

'No, I didn't let him go,' he said. 'I asked him if he would mind waiting a few minutes. And then your Sergeant told him that he knew you would like a word with him.'

Inspector Grant looked relieved at this news. 'That's good,' he said, rubbing his hands together in a satisfied manner. 'Bring him in here right away, will you, Mr. Denham?'

As he went to the door the Manager explained. 'He says his name is Bennett. I'll get him and send him in to you, Inspector, right away.'

Miss Frayle looked duly impressed by the way in which Inspector Grant was handling the case. 'You think that he may be able to tell us something about Miss Donetti, and what has happened to her, Inspector?' she asked.

'Maybe,' the Inspector said. 'That is, of course, if he will tell us what he knows. But then, perhaps you'll be able to persuade him to tell us a thing or two, Doctor.'

125

Doctor Morelle smiled sardonically. 'That,' he said, 'depends in essence upon whether or no he has anything to conceal. After all, we must bear in mind that as yet we have no information whatsoever on that not unimportant point.'

Bennett, when he came in, proved to be a middle-aged man of quite ordinary appearance, dressed in a dark lounge suit and carrying a raincoat over one arm. He looked a little surprised at what was happening.

'What's all this about, gentlemen?' he remarked as he entered. 'I came along here to call on Miss Donetti, and I seem somehow to have got myself mixed up with some police matter. Can you tell me what is happening?'

Inspector Grant knew how to deal with this sort of approach.

'Sorry to trouble you, Mr. Bennett,' he said in soothing tones, 'but it so happens that we are rather interested in the lady whose name you mentioned. As she isn't here to speak for herself, we wondered if perhaps you might have some information about her, which would enable us to fill in the gaps in our knowledge. This, incidentally, is Miss Frayle, and this is Doctor Morelle.'

Bennett looked at Doctor Morelle. His jaw dropped, as if he had been very surprised. Then he smiled at Miss Frayle. She giggled and nodded. There seemed to be a sense of embarrassment and tenseness in the air.

'This,' Inspector Grant went on, 'is Molly O'Brien. She is Miss Donetti's maid, and she has been able to give us a certain amount of information about her employer.'

'Good evening, sir,' Molly said, with a smile which mixed demureness and pertness.

The Inspector was studying Bennett's face with some care as he made these introductions. It seemed that the detective thought that it was possible that the man in some way might give himself away when faced by the others. But such was not the case. Bennett did not give any sign of perturbation.

'Possibly, though,' Inspector Grant said, 'you have already met Miss O'Brien during your period of friendship, or acquaintanceship, with Miss Donetti?'

Bennett shook his head decisively. 'I'm afraid not,' he pointed out. 'As a matter of fact, you see, I've never even met Miss Donetti myself yet.'

This was quite clearly a considerable surprise to Inspector Grant, and possibly he was a trifle disappointed also. This, however, he did not reveal in an open way.

He merely raised his eyebrows slightly and glanced at Doctor Morelle.

The Doctor said, in rasping tones: 'Indeed? Then I am afraid, Mr. Bennett, that the doubtful pleasure of meeting her is something of which you will have to face the postponement. I trust that it will not cause you too much pain.'

The Inspector smiled gently at this sally, and resumed his cross-examination with the question: 'What exactly were you wanting to see Miss Donetti about tonight, Mr. Bennett?'

Bennett hesitated before replying. It appeared as if he was conscious that here he was skating upon thin ice, and was very doubtful of just what reply would be both truthful and tactful. He coughed and shuffled his feet.

Then he said: 'Well, I suppose there's no reason why you shouldn't have the truth about the business. The fact of the matter is that I deal in jewellery — valuable stuff, you know — in a small way. I'm an amateur, and make quite a hobby out of buying and selling small pieces. Miss Donetti sent me a message that she had some jewellery she wanted to dispose of. She asked me if I would call here tonight, about this time, when she hoped to be able to show me some stuff, which she thought would interest me. That was all it amounted to, and that is why I was so surprised when I found that she wasn't available.'

Doctor Morelle listened to this description with a smile of withering scepticism on his lips. He was obviously not in any way impressed by what Bennett had told them.

'How did Miss Donetti come to hear of you and your amateur efforts at dealing in jewellery, Mr. Bennett?' he asked, and there was more than a hint of sarcasm in his tone which did not escape Bennett's attention.

Bennett waved his hand airily. 'I'm quite well known around here,' he said,

'Indeed?' queried Doctor Morelle. 'You are a resident in Hull of some long standing, then?'

'Oh, yes,' Bennett replied suavely. 'I've lived here for some ten years or so.'

'But your deals are purely private affairs, aren't they?' asked the Inspector.

'Yes, quite private. But these things get known. You can't keep them altogether to yourself. And anybody who wants to do a deal soon gets to hear of me, you know.'

Doctor Morelle still looked sceptical.

'And you wish to imply that this is how Miss Donetti got to know of you, no doubt?' he asked.

Bennett grinned. 'Well, as I have already said, I'd never met her, and I assumed that she had been put on to me by some mutual friend who knew about my deals in jewellery, and thought that Miss Donetti and I might find each other useful. That is the explanation that I can give you, and I don't know of any other. If you have any different suggestion to make, I shall be pleased to say if I think it at all likely.'

The Inspector stroked his chin thoughtfully. This, it appeared, was not the kind of explanation that he had anticipated, but he realized that it was a moderately convincing story, and one that would not be at all easy to disprove. Leaving Bennett for a moment, he turned to Molly O'Brien.

'Did you know that this gentleman would be calling to see Miss Donetti tonight?' he asked the maid.

'I'd no notion of it,' she replied. 'Miss Donetti said nothing to me about anyone calling. But then she didn't tell me anything about her private affairs, as I told you just now.'

'Were you aware,' Doctor Morelle interjected, 'that your employer had in her possession some jewellery, which she was desirous of selling to Mr. Bennett or to anyone else?'

'She never told me,' Molly persisted stubbornly. 'I know nothing at all about her business or her private affairs.'

The Inspector had now made up his mind. It was clear to him that the moment for action had come. And Inspector Grant was a man of action who did not hesitate to move when it was clear to him that the circumstances demanded movement.

'Mr. Bennett,' he said thoughtfully, 'I wonder if you'd mind popping along to the station with me so that I could check up on one or two points, and get a statement written out, which you could then sign? You see, we are very anxious to get in touch with Miss Donetti, and you are possibly the only person available at the moment who can assist us in our search for her.'

Bennett looked slightly alarmed. 'Surely,' he said, 'that isn't altogether necessary, Inspector. I've told you all I know. As I have said, I never met Miss Donetti, and I think it's very unlikely that anything I can do will help you to find her. Besides, my wife is waiting for me at home. It's getting late, and she'll be very anxious if I keep her waiting very much longer. You know what the ladies are like.'

'Yes, indeed,' said Miss Frayle in her usual sympathetic way.

'Is your wife on the 'phone?' the Inspector asked quietly.

'Yes,' Bennett replied.

The Inspector smiled. 'That's all right, then,' he said. 'You can just ring her up and let her know that you are having a chat with the police. Explain that it's nothing serious, and that you expect to be home in an hour or two.'

'It's all a bit of a nuisance,' Bennett grumbled. 'Still, if you insist, Inspector.'

He fumbled in his pocket, fished out a handful of money, and said: 'Is there a call-box anywhere about, do you know?'

'Yes,' answered Miss Frayle. 'There is one just by the reception desk. It's one of those slot things, you know.'

'Have I got any coppers?' Bennett murmured. 'Only one penny, I'm afraid. Can anyone lend me another penny, please?'

Miss Frayle opened her handbag, looked in it for a moment, produced a coin, and handed it over.

'There you are, Mr. Bennett,' she said with a smile.

'Thanks very much,' Bennett replied, smiling in his turn. 'I'll pay you back, you know.' He made his way to the door, saying as he went, 'I won't be a minute, then, Inspector. It's only a local call, so it will only take a moment to put through. Then I'll be right back again.'

Doctor Morelle had been watching the proceedings carefully for the last few minutes. Now he held up his hand in a minatory gesture.

'I think that you'd better stay right where you are, Mr. Bennett!' he exclaimed. 'Before you go out to telephone you have a considerable amount of explaining to do.'

'What do you mean?' Bennett expostulated.

'Yes; what's the idea, Doctor?' asked Inspector Grant in considerable surprise.

'Merely that I suspect this man knows a good deal more about this Donetti person than he has so far admitted,' said Doctor Morelle slowly. 'I think that you should ask him some more questions before you allow him to leave our presence.'

Miss Frayle put her hand to her mouth. 'Look out, Inspector!' she screamed.

Indeed, Bennett was making for the door as fast as he could go.

'No you don't!' Inspector Grant exclaimed, hurling himself rapidly across the room. 'You stay put, my man! I want to know a good deal more about you than you've yet told me.'

He grabbed the man by the arm, and Bennett wriggled madly in the attempt to get rid of the detective's grip. But Inspector Grant had graduated in a hard school — the school of dockland — and he was used to almost every kind of rough-house.

'Blast you!' grunted Bennett. 'Keep your hands off me.'

'I shouldn't struggle if I were you,' the Inspector said. 'You might get hurt. You come along quietly to the station, and everything will be all right. Otherwise I don't know what might happen.'

'If you will kindly remain here, Miss Frayle,' Doctor Morelle said, 'I will accompany Inspector Grant and his guest to the Police Station. I do not anticipate that I shall be absent for more than half an hour or so, and when I return I shall doubtless be able to satisfy that inordinate curiosity as to the course of events in Hull which is no doubt, at this precise moment, so agitating your restless mind.'

The next half-hour seemed a long time to Miss Frayle. She sat down and tried to read, but she found her attention wandering from the book. Then she walked up and down the lounge, but found that all the time one insistent question was hammering in her mind. If it was true that Bennett was an accomplice of Miss Donetti — and his behaviour seemed to place that beyond all doubt — how had Doctor Morelle realized the fact? The doctor always said that every criminal made a mistake, and the alert mind should be able to spot that mistake. Miss Frayle could only conclude that her mind was not efficiently alert for the purpose.

At length, however, the Doctor returned.

He looked more than ordinarily pleased with himself, and as he came in he was rubbing his hands together in a satisfied manner.

'I think that we have performed a very satisfactory evening's work, my dear Miss Frayle,' he said.

'Why, what happened at the Police Station?' she asked

'Under interrogation by the estimable Inspector Grant, Bennett revealed that he was indeed an accomplice of the Donetti woman. He has divulged an address in the South of England where she can be found, and I have no doubt that within a matter of hours at most both she and sundry other confederates will be duly apprehended and incarcerated under lock and key.'

'It's an astonishing piece of work Doctor!' Miss Frayle said.

'Moderately simple, though,' the Doctor added in self-satisfied tones.

'I must say,' added Miss Frayle, 'that it was pretty smart of you to catch on to the fact that he really had no intention of 'phoning his wife, but was merely using the 'phone call as an excuse to make a getaway.'

'His request for the loan of a second penny is what made me quite certain of his complicity in the crime,' Doctor Morelle explained patiently.

'I don't see why,' Miss Frayle objected. 'After all, everyone knows that you have to put twopence in a public telephone in order to make a local call.'

'On the contrary,' Doctor Morelle corrected her, 'that request for a second penny proved the complete falsity of his earlier claim that he was an old resident of Hull — of, if I remember aright, ten years standing.'

Miss Frayle was puzzled. 'But why, Doctor?' she asked in a bewildered way. 'What did it prove?'

'It proved that he could have been in Hull for only a comparatively short time,' the Doctor said.

'Why?'

'The charge for a local call from a public telephone booth in this city, my dear Miss Frayle, is one penny only.'

Miss Frayle looked more surprised

than ever. 'Is that really so, Doctor?' she asked.

'Indubitably,' the Doctor replied.

'How you find out these things is what amazes me!' Miss Frayle exclaimed.

'The fact has been fairly widely publicised of late in the columns of the national Press,' Doctor Morelle said in complacent tones. 'Those who do not confine themselves to the more sensational headlines and the advertisements of the more erotic types of films would have noted the report.'

'You wouldn't be taking a dig at me, would you?' asked Miss Frayle with a giggle. The Doctor ignored this remark.

'It is true,' he went on, 'that my superior acumen enabled me to discern the fatal error which was made by Bennett under cross-examination. The error would doubtless have escaped notice had I been a person of merely average intelligence.'

Miss Frayle smiled. 'There is one other question I have been meaning to ask you ever since we came to Hull, Doctor Morelle,' she said.

'Yes, my dear Miss Frayle,' he answered, now quite complacent, since the case had been brought to such a satisfactory conclusion. 'What further information would you wish me to vouchsafe you?'

'You remember,' she said, 'that you came down here to advise on a case of paranoia.'

'Precisely.'

'What exactly does the word paranoia mean? I've been wondering ever since we arrived.'

Doctor Morelle snorted impatiently. 'It is a perfectly ordinary word, in general use in the medical profession, Miss Frayle,' he replied. 'It means chronic delusive obsession with one's own self-importance.'

Miss Frayle giggled. 'Ah!' she exclaimed. 'I thought it was something of the sort. That explains it.'

'Explains what, may I ask?' snarled the Doctor.

'Why they called *you* into consultation,' murmured Miss Frayle.

3

The Case of the Man in the Car

Freda Hopkins had never liked her name. As soon as she left her secondary school, she contrived to add a letter to her Christian name. 'Frieda' was much more distinctive, redolent of some foreign origin, suggestive perhaps of a chateau on the Danube or a cabaret in Budapest. She clung tenaciously to 'Frieda', and her ever-growing circle of male admirers was duly impressed. It seemed to fit in with her tawny hair, grey-green eyes and slightly mysterious air.

Since her father's death, Frieda had travelled around quite a lot with her mother, who had a fair-sized private income. They favoured resorts such as Bournemouth, Southport, Leamington and Buxton, where there was a certain amount of congenial company for Mrs. Hopkins, and a fair supply of eligible males for Frieda. For nearly four years, she danced, played tennis, flirted and generally frittered away time to her heart's content. But she still disliked her second name. True, one or two of her more serious admirers had suggested that she might care to change it, but on careful inquiry from Mrs. Hopkins they had proved singularly lacking in this world's goods; indeed two of them were under the distinct impression that Frieda had a substantial income which could be accommodated to the needs of a penniless husband. In fact, none of her various young male friends seemed to be over-blessed with riches, and Frieda had to have money.

'My daughter is accustomed to a certain standard of living,' Mrs. Hopkins would inform would-be suitors in a dignified tone that was always sufficient to deter the most ardent of them. It was not until Mrs. Hopkins took a small furnished flat at Worthing, and began to entertain Frieda's friends in a slightly more domesticated style that she began to attract the rather more dependable type of man.

Among them was Malcolm Sutcliffe, a prosperous chartered accountant from Sevenoaks, where he had inherited a thriving business from his uncle. He was ten years older than Frieda, but Mrs. Hopkins dismissed this as the merest bagatelle, and threw them into each other's company as frequently as possible. After Malcolm's week's holiday was over, he continued to motor down to Worthing quite frequently at weekends, and on Frieda's twenty-first birthday, their engagement was announced.

Mrs. Hopkins' death following a seizure hastened their marriage, and within the year, Frieda found herself mistress of a charming imitation Tudor residence, standing in three acres of grounds in the little village of Dockham, five miles from Sevenoaks, in the midst of a wooded hillside.

For the first few months, the novelty of her new life absorbed her completely. Malcolm had a fairly wide circle of friends, who were quite interesting at first acquaintance, but whom she later came to regard as dull in the extreme. Frieda had not much affinity with the business-man type or his wife. She began to wonder why she had married Malcolm, regretting that she had not first travelled around a little longer, enjoying the untramelled benefit of the money her mother had left to her.

She dismissed Malcolm's friends as 'poor sports'. Indeed, the only person of her acquaintance whom she classed as a 'good sport' was a young man named Lloyd Bradbury, whom she had first met in his capacity as second cashier to the Kentish County Bank at Sevenoaks. After her third visit they had reached a stage of familiarity which seemed to warrant her inviting him over to Dorkham for the evening — she made sure it would be a Wednesday, when Malcolm always spent the evening at the golf club. Young Bradbury had always belonged to that class of bank clerks who mix with their social superiors at all costs — which accounts for the fact that every member of the Big Five banks averages a case a day of embezzlement.

Bradbury considered himself in clover

at 'Three Gables', Dorkham. Not only was his hostess a very personable and charming young woman, not averse to what he described as 'a bit of fun', but there was also a selection of free drinks, which delighted his heart and considerably relieved his pocket, for most of his spare money found its way into hotel tills.

After his second visit, Frieda casually included him in a small party she was giving, and he met her husband, who considered him a very pleasant young man and thought very little more about him at the time. He made no comment when he frequently returned home to find Bradbury sprawled in his favourite armchair, or occupying the hard court with Frieda. They had been married four years now, and he had an ever-growing connection to keep him occupied: in fact there was some talk between himself and his cousin of buying up a firm in Frome which had discreetly approached them through a third party. Yes, Malcolm certainly had plenty to keep his mind occupied. And he always boasted that he and Frieda trusted each other.

That the affair between Lloyd Bradbury and Frieda Sutcliffe was the topic of a hundred tea tables in and around Sevenoaks would appear to have escaped him, and it might well have gently fizzled out as had so many of Frieda's early romances. But for the first time in her life, Frieda discovered that she was in love, at least as far as her shallow nature was capable of any such emotion. And Lloyd Bradbury was so highly infatuated with her that he too concluded it must be 'the real thing'.

Even now, all would have been well if they had maintained a bare minimum of discretion. But they seemed proud of their attachment; flaunted it defiantly beneath the noses of the county matrons and local squires. Naturally the latter considered it their duty to acquaint Malcolm Sutcliffe, who was generally liked, with the current state of affairs. One or two of them even spoke to Lloyd Bradbury's manager, who summoned the young cashier to his office and laid down the law in no uncertain fashion. But Bradbury paid no heed; he knew the bank had no real jurisdiction over his leisure hours, as long as he did his job capably.

When Sutcliffe taxed Frieda on the subject, she was downright defiant, refused to give up Bradbury, and when her husband declared that he would forbid him to enter the house, retorted that she would then be under the necessity of visiting Bradbury — at his flat in Sevenoaks.

'Very well,' said Malcolm quietly. 'I won't forbid him the house. We'll simply leave the district. Then you'll soon get over this infatuation.'

She could hardly believe her ears.

'Malcolm — what do you mean? How can we leave the district?' she gasped incredulously.

'I shall go and supervise the new branch at Frome,' he told her.

'Then I shall stay here.'

'Oh no you won't. I propose to let this house furnished,' he announced with a quiet decision that amazed her.

'I'll stay by myself in the district,' she retorted.

He shook his head.

'I don't think so, because you see under those circumstances I couldn't make you any allowance.'

She knew she was defeated. Her mother's income had stopped at her death, and the few hundreds she had left to Frieda had somehow slipped away in the intervening years.

'But Malcolm — ' she began to protest.

'There's nothing more to be said,' he replied coldly, and went across to the telephone.

'What are you going to do?' she asked in some trepidation.

'Telephone Roger Ludlow and put the house in his hands right away.'

She turned and rushed from the room in a blazing fury, ran upstairs and flung herself on the bed, sobbing hysterically.

* * *

A week later, Doctor Morelle and Miss Frayle were sitting in Roger Ludlow's office. He was looking for a country house on a short lease to enable him to enjoy a change of air, and also to conduct a certain amount of chemical research without any intrusion. He had always liked the wooded slopes and fertile valleys of this part of Kent, and it seemed that many others shared this preference.

'I'm afraid I have only one suitable residence on the books,' sighed the agent, a pudgy young man, who looked ten years older than his actual age. 'And that's only just come onto the market — it'll soon be snapped up too. I know it pretty well; the owner's quite a friend of mine. Lovely position — stands well on a hill — see for miles — every convenience — four good rooms downstairs — five bedrooms — two bathrooms — '

He paused to take a breath and handed over a photograph.

'Here you are, Doctor. Take a look at this picture.'

'H'm . . . ' murmured the Doctor. 'Not unprepossessing in appearance. Is it possible to obtain possession in the near future?'

'Within the next few weeks. The owner is moving to Frome temporarily — but he tells me he expects to return possibly in about six months' time. That is why there's only a short lease available.'

'That would suit me admirably,' agreed the Doctor, passing on the photograph to Miss Frayle.

'You'll find it well worth the trouble of inspection,' Ludlow assured them. 'In fact, it's liable to be snapped up any time.'

'Yes, do let's go and see it, Doctor,' put in Miss Frayle rather too eagerly for his liking.

'The owner will permit you to view any time you wish — within reason of course,' Ludlow informed them.

'I do not propose to inspect the property in the middle of the night,' replied Doctor Morelle with a wintry smile.

'Quite,' agreed Ludlow hurriedly. 'I'm sure you'll find it quite ideal for your purpose if you allow me to make an appointment.'

'Can't we go along now?' demanded the persistent Miss Frayle. 'It would save us another journey down here.'

The Doctor agreed with her for once.

'If you will excuse me a moment,' said the agent, 'I'll telephone the house, just to make sure either Mr. or Mrs. Sutcliffe is at home, and let them know we're coming along. It'll only take us about twenty minutes in the car — extremely convenient for shopping, you see . . . '

When they reached 'Three Gables', about half-an-hour later, a well-built young man with dark, wavy hair and heavy features was just coming out of the front door. He entered his rather battered saloon car and drove away without acknowledging their arrival, so the Doctor presumed that he could not be the owner of the house.

The Doctor observed that Ludlow's reaction to the young man's presence was a tiny frown, and then an expression of blank indifference.

They climbed out of the car, and entered the neat brick porch with its heavily studded front door. Ludlow rang the bell, and the door was opened almost at once by a striking young woman whom he addressed as Mrs. Sutcliffe.

She appeared to be quite pleased to see

them, called Mr. Ludlow by his Christian name, and invited them inside.

'I'm so sorry my husband isn't here,' she apologised. 'He went out to see a friend just before you telephoned.'

'I explained to Doctor Morelle and Miss Frayle,' said Ludlow. 'However, Mrs. Sutcliffe, no doubt you would be able to conduct us over the house.'

'It's awfully attractive — and the garden's really lovely,' supplemented Miss Frayle.

'I am glad you like it,' smiled Mrs. Sutcliffe. 'We've spent quite a lot of money there.' She led the way out of the neatly panelled entrance hall through an archway.

'This is a sort of lounge,' she began, moving across towards the French windows. 'We generally have our meals in this recess. There's a serving-hatch to the kitchen.'

'That's very useful,' commented Miss Frayle.

They made an exhaustive tour of the house, which was substantially built, well-decorated, and if some of the modern furniture had rather an uncomfortable aspect, the Doctor had to admit himself impressed by the general layout of the house. Miss Frayle was frankly enthusiastic.

'Thank you so much for showing us this beautiful home of yours,' she said politely when the tour was complete.

'Yes, we're very grateful,' added Ludlow, a little breathless from climbing stairs. 'Pity Malcolm isn't here . . . '

'I can't think where he's got to — he should be back any minute,' she replied.

'Perhaps if we walked around the grounds and surveyed the three acres you advertise,' suggested the Doctor, 'your husband will have returned by then.'

'Yes — yes, of course,' she agreed. 'Roger, would you mind taking Doctor Morelle and Miss Frayle over the grounds and the paddock? I have rather an urgent 'phone call to make — I'll join you presently.'

'Certainly, Mrs. Sutcliffe,' agreed Ludlow with alacrity.

'You can go out this way.' She opened the French windows for them.

When they were outside, Doctor Morelle turned to Ludlow, and asked:

'There is a garage, I presume?'

'Of course — jolly good garage — I've left my car in there several times. Room for three cars if they're not too big. This way . . . '

They approached the front doors of the garage. Ludlow went to open them, but they were locked.

'That's queer,' he mused. 'Malcolm doesn't generally lock them up when he's out with the car.'

'Perhaps he didn't take the car,' suggested Miss Frayle.

Ludlow pushed his hat to the back of his head.

'From what I remember,' he said thoughtfully, 'the back doors are usually only on a catch . . . they're in two sections, and the top half comes open easily.'

They went round to the rear, and the agent began pulling at the top half of the doors. Almost immediately, they noticed a strong smell of petrol fumes, and as the doors opened a wave of exhaust gas swept towards them.

'Stand back a moment!' ordered the Doctor, covering his face with his handkerchief.

'Whatever can have happened?' coughed Miss Frayle.

They could see now that there was a car in the garage.

'Somebody must have left the engine running,' spluttered Ludlow. 'It's Malcolm's car . . . I thought he'd taken it . . . '

'The engine was left running for a very definite purpose,' announced Doctor Morelle grimly indicating a man's form slumped over the wheel. It was the form of a slim man in his thirties, a slight tonsure showing as his head pitched forward.

'My God! It's Malcolm Sutcliffe!' gasped the agent, clasping the back of the car for support.

By a supreme effort of will, Miss Frayle choked back a scream.

'What a ghastly sight!' whispered the agent, his pudgy features assuming a bluish tinge. He grasped ineffectively at the smooth back of the saloon, then sank slowly to the ground.

'Doctor Morelle, he's fainted!' cried Miss Frayle.

'So I observe,' said the Doctor in some astonishment. 'It is usually *your* prerogative, Miss Frayle.'

'I — I don't feel very well,' she admitted, in what he imagined sounded rather a hopeful tone.

'Pull yourself together, Miss Frayle. This is not the first time in your life that you have been confronted by a body or bodies. Let us examine this one in the car . . . '

The air had cleared considerably now, and he was able to remove his handkerchief and bend over the inert form of Malcolm Sutcllffe.

'H'm . . . a case of carbon monoxide asphyxiation,' he announced after a very brief examination.

'Poor man,' whispered Miss Frayle. 'I suppose it must have been an accident.'

He looked up, somewhat surprised. 'Ah, Miss Frayle, I had taken it for granted that you had assumed your customary horizontal posture by this time.'

'I'm feeling better,' declared Miss Frayle defiantly.

'The Kentish air must agree with you. I wonder how much petrol is left in this tank?'

'Doesn't the gauge there show?' she asked.

'That indicates zero — because the engine has stopped.'

'Shall I have a look in the tank?' she offered.

'Yes, I've no doubt you could see with the aid of a lighted match.'

'Isn't that rather dangerous?' she demanded innocently.

'Remain where you are. I will ascertain the amount of petrol remaining by switching on the engine. The gauge will react accordingly.'

He turned to the dashboard, only to find the ignition key missing. He searched the pigeonholes and the pockets of the car without success, then produced the key to his own car.

'Doubtless, this will fit,' he murmured.

The engine spluttered into life, ran for a moment, then choked to a standstill.

'Is it all right, Doctor?' Miss Frayle asked.

'Perfectly. The petrol supply has not been exhausted — nearly two gallons remain.'

Doctor Morelle withdrew the key, replaced it in his pocket, and crossed swiftly to where Roger Ludlow lay in an awkward position. Quickly, he loosened his collar.

The agent moaned.

'What happened?' he whispered, slowly recovering consciousness. Then he seemed to recall everything, and groaned again.

'Poor man,' said Miss Frayle. 'Perhaps if I got some water . . . '

'I took the liberty of extracting this brandy flask from the car,' said the Doctor. 'He will probably need it when I impart a certain piece of information. The shock may be considerable.'

'Another shock?' queried Miss Frayle in a puzzled voice.

'When I inform him that Mr. Sutcllffe has been murdered,' declared the Doctor deliberately.

'Murdered!' gasped Miss Frayle. 'Oh,

Doctor . . . oh . . . '

There was a moan and a slight thud as she subsided against the garage wall.

'Stupid, incalculable young woman,' snapped Doctor Morelle testily. 'Why on earth should she want to faint now?'

★   ★   ★

They drove back to Sevenoaks, after breaking the news to Mrs. Sutcliffe, who reacted even more violently than they had anticipated. She screamed, shook her husband's inert form, fainted, recovered, screamed again and relapsed into hysterics. It had taken them the better part of an hour to restore her. Roger Ludlow, sitting beside the Doctor, who was driving, seemed badly shaken by his experiences of the afternoon, and Miss Frayle in the back seat was rather white, and still clung to the small bottle of smelling-salts she always carried round in her bag.

'You didn't tell Mrs. Sutcliffe her husband was murdered,' said Roger Ludlow at length.

'There seemed to be no point in arousing her to further histrionic display,' replied the Doctor acidly.

The agent eyed him incredulously.

'You — you don't think she had anything to do with it?' he stammered.

The Doctor kept his eyes on the road ahead.

'At the moment, I prefer to make no conjecture until I have laid certain facts before the police,' he answered. They hardly spoke again until the car drew up outside the police station. After they had each made a brief deposition, Doctor Morelle went into conference with the Inspector in charge.

* * *

'I still can't think how you can make such a rash statement,' said Miss Frayle pensively, as they drove back to London.

'To what are you referring?'

'Saying that poor man was murdered. You had no real evidence.'

'On the contrary,' he snapped, 'there was most conclusive evidence. The car was not of unusual manufacture, and the engine must have been started by an ignition key. That key was missing, however, and in order to test the petrol gauge by starting the car, I had to use my own. This was conclusive proof that someone had, after running the engine, returned subsequently and removed the key which he had used for the purpose.'

'Well, yes, perhaps you're right . . . ' she conceded with some reluctance. Then her face lit up. 'Doctor . . . that young man who was leaving the house . . . it looked very much the same sort of car . . . '

'I have already notified the police to that effect,' he calmly informed her. 'At this moment, he is undergoing an intensive cross-examination. The Inspector told me there is a certain association between this young man and Mrs. Sutcliffe, so he will, doubtless, not have far to seek for a motive.

'It's all very regrettable,' sighed the Doctor, after a further pause.

'Then you're sorry for her? I thought she was attractive, too.'

'I am referring to our failure to

conclude negotiations for the lease of the house,' he retorted bitingly.

'But the place may be on the market — she wouldn't want to stay there now,' she said brightening. 'Even if she's proved innocent . . . '

He turned and swept her with a pitying glance.

'My dear Miss Frayle, you do not appear to appreciate that this trial will probably prove as highly sensational as any since that of Doctor Crippen. The house we have just seen will be a mecca for trippers from all over England. Perhaps you would welcome the opportunity to show them round at a shilling a head!'

She subsided and said no more until they reached the outskirts of London. Then she sighed.

'I'm rather glad we're not going to live there after all,' she told him.

'And why, pray?'

'Because,' explained Miss Frayle with a shiver, 'the house is almost certain to be haunted!'

4

The Case of the Insured Jewels

It was natural, as a result of the great reputation which he had acquired, that Doctor Morelle should from time to time be called to attend to the great and the famous, in all walks of life. Miss Frayle sometimes regretted that she had not, when starting her work with the Doctor some years earlier, brought with her an autograph book in which, with care, she could have amassed a collection of signatures which would have been unique in the history of autographs and which, at the same time, would have been extremely valuable. Famous writers, scientists, and artists came along with an almost monotonous regularity; film stars, from the great Carol James downwards, were almost weekly visitors to the Doctor's unpretentious house; and leaders in politics and industry, though not so frequent as those in the artistic professions, often called to see the Doctor on some obscure nervous disorder. There were occasions, also, on which princes and princesses came along — for it was but rarely that the Doctor could be persuaded to go and see them unless he was assured either that it was a matter of life and death or that one of his beloved criminological problems were involved.

Yet to Miss Frayle, with her sympathetic outlook on the problems of suffering humanity, nothing was more interesting than the procession of diverse human beings which made its way, day by day, through the consulting room. She thought that they were really fascinating in their diversity.

One of the most fascinating women that the Doctor had ever attended, Miss Frayle thought, was Mrs. Halsted, whose husband was by way of being an important person in business circles in the city of London — to wit, managing director of the Blue Star Insurance Company. She had been suffering from a nervous disorder which had baffled many doctors who were supposed to be expert in such matters. Yet Doctor Morelle had succeeded in diagnosing it, and, without much difficulty (so it appeared to Miss Frayle), had brought about a cure so surprising that to the sufferer and her husband it seemed to be something almost miraculous. The Doctor's account of the matter in the *Lancet*, which appeared some months later, was destined to become almost a classic in the annals of nervous disease.

It was therefore with some surprise that the Doctor, who was very busy dictating to Miss Frayle one morning a few weeks after the successful determination of Mrs. Halsted's illness, found that Mr. Halsted was waiting to see him.

When Halsted came in Doctor Morelle looked at him with some curiosity. He thought that there was a definite appearance of anxiety in the man's eyes, and he at once offered Halsted a seat and waited for some revelation as to the reason why he was once more being consulted.

'It's very good of you to see me again, Doctor Morelle,' Halsted said. 'I often read of your activities, and I know of your very extensive practice, so I know what an extremely busy man you must be.'

Miss Frayle looked at the man with human interest and sympathy. Her eyes had tears in them as she recalled the mental state in which Mrs. Halsted had recently been.

'I hope that your wife is getting on all right now, Mr. Halsted,' she said.

Halsted smiled a rather wan smile. 'Thank you, Miss Frayle,' he replied, and then corrected himself. 'Or rather, thanks to Doctor Morelle here,' he added, 'she's doing fine. There's no trace of any return of the old trouble.'

Doctor Morelle had been studying the man with care while this conversation was going on. Now he said: 'You yourself do not appear to be in any need of *medical* attention, Mr. Halsted. Skin clear, hand steady, eyes a little strained perhaps . . . ' He paused and turned to his amenuensis. 'Ah, yes,' he exclaimed with the air of a man who has made a great discovery. 'Miss Frayle?'

Miss Frayle woke out of the daydream

into which Halsted's remarks about his wife had plunged her. 'Yes, Doctor,' she said in her absent-minded manner.

'Take some notes. if you can regain your normal composure sufficiently to undertake any such mundane activity.' There was a clear-cut air of decision about the Doctor's manner, which at once told Miss Frayle that he had come to a definite conclusion with regard to the reason why Halsted had decided to visit the consulting room on this morning.

'Notes, Doctor?' Miss Frayle said, in simulated surprise. 'Notes about what?'

'Notes about the matter which Mr. Halsted wishes to discuss with us.'

'And that is . . . ?' Miss Frayle was unable to give the Doctor the opportunity of showing off his brilliance of deduction in such a matter.

'I have no doubt that he is about to ask my advice with regard to the fate of some valuable jewellery which was lost, in somewhat mysterious circumstances a week ago,' the Doctor said with a smile of triumph that might almost be described as a smirk, if the Doctor had not been too dignified a person ever to indulge in that extremely undignified gesture.

Halsted looked at the Doctor in the most complete amazement. His eyes gaped, his mouth opened wide. There was something almost comic about his surprise.

'Great Scott, Doctor!' he exclaimed. 'How on earth did you guess what I . . . ?'

'As I recall it,' Doctor Morelle went on, 'the individual who apparently mislaid the gems is named Helen Blane, a professional actress.'

If Halsted had been surprised before, he was now practically speechless with amazement. He managed to gasp out the words: 'This is amazing!'

Miss Frayle was equally impressed. She had, in her time with Doctor Morelle, seen many extraordinarily impressive examples of his almost uncanny mental powers; but this was perhaps the most impressive of them all.

'How have you managed to guess it, Doctor Morelle?' she asked, her eyes wide open with astonishment.

There was a sneering tone in the

Doctor's voice as he replied: 'My dear Miss Frayle,' he said, 'you have surely been in association with me long enough now to know that I never indulge in that pernicious habit known as guessing. When I am faced with a problem, no matter how difficult it may appear to be on the surface, I do not guess; I deduce.'

Halsted still looked surprised, however. 'Not a soul, I thought, knew that I was coming to consult you about the disappearance of those jewels,' he said.

Doctor Morelle took a deep breath, as if he was containing himself with great difficulty. Then he went on, explaining with an attitude of restraint: 'You have informed us that your wife is still in perfect health, I can easily see for myself that you are reasonably well, though possibly a little over-anxious about something as yet undisclosed by you. Therefore it is obvious that it is not any medical matter about which you have approached me.'

'That's true enough,' Halsted agreed.

'And, since I have in recent years acquired what I may describe, I think, as a considerable reputation in dealing with criminological matters, I may take it that it is in some way in connection with a crime that you wish to consult me.'

Halsted looked not altogether convinced by this analysis of the position.

'But I still don't quite see how you decided that it was in connection with the jewels of Miss Blane that I wanted to see you, Doctor,' he argued.

Doctor Morelle smiled. 'It is surely obvious enough,' he said. 'You are managing director of a large and important insurance company. I noticed in the Press last week a report of the loss of the precious stones in question. I assume that the insurance company concerned — your own — will have to pay a considerable sum in settlement of the claim. Naturally, if there is any doubt about the way in which the stones disappeared, you will want to have the matter investigated by one who may be described as an expert in crime — which, I suggest, is a description which can not unfairly be applied to myself.'

Halsted laughed. 'Pretty good, Doctor,'

he said, 'Your deductions are, of course, absolutely correct.'

'I must say, Doctor Morelle,' Miss Frayle added, her eyes fairly glowing with excitement and admiration for her employer, 'that really is most awfully smart of you!'

'Thank you, my dear Miss Frayle,' replied the Doctor with a slight bow. But there was an undercurrent of sarcasm in his voice that she did not altogether like.

Halsted's handsome face set, however, in an expression of grim determination. 'But seriously, Doctor,' he said, 'this is a pretty important matter for me. And I need your help badly, I must admit. This time it is not on my wife's behalf, but on my own — or rather, my firm's.'

Doctor Morelle nodded gravely. He realized readily enough that even the greatest insurance companies would not be ready to pay out a sum as great as that involved in this case unless the whole matter were submitted to the most stringent investigation.

'What precisely,' the Doctor asked quietly, 'is this actress person's status in her somewhat disreputable profession?'

'She's famous for her lovely red hair!' exclaimed Miss Frayle, without any apparent reason.

'I am not,' Doctor Morelle pointed out, 'enquiring after her pulchritudinous assets — if red hair of that particular type may justifiably be regarded as an asset.'

'I think it may!' Miss Frayle exclaimed with an ecstatic smile. 'In fact, I have often wondered whether it wouldn't be as well for me to try . . . '

'Miss Frayle,' snapped the Doctor, 'kindly refrain from bringing your beauty parlour vanities into this discussion, which, I would remind you, is concerned with the disappearance of some jewellery and not with the alleged beauties of an actress.'

Halsted had listened to this exchange of remarks with a smile, though his own feelings were serious enough, as he had already indicated.

'Miss Blane is a cabaret star,' he explained, 'although I must say, Doctor, that I think she could be better described as notorious than as famous.'

Doctor Morelle's expression showed his distaste with cabaret stars. 'Personally,' he said, 'I should describe all such seekers after the limelight and vulgar sensationalism as notorious rather than famous.'

Miss Frayle smiled secretly to herself. 'You are hardly a blushing violet yourself,' she murmured, scarcely realizing that she had spoken her thoughts aloud.

'You said something, I think, Miss Frayle?' the Doctor said, rounding sharply on her.

'Nothing, nothing,' Miss Frayle replied, regretting that she had allowed herself to speak aloud.

'I thought that I heard you make some remark about violets,' Doctor Morelle pursued.

'I merely remarked that I was very fond of violets,' Miss Frayle remarked, trying to get out of the awkward position in which her indiscreet words had landed her. She felt that the Doctor was still more than a trifle suspicious, although outwardly he showed no sign of having any knowledge of what she had actually said.

'A remark singularly inane, in that it

has no connection with the matter which is at present under discussion,' he said.

'I'm in a very awkward spot, Doctor Morelle, and I'm hoping that you will be able to do something to help,' Halsted explained.

'What is the particular difficulty which faces you at the moment?' Doctor Morelle asked.

'I just can't call in the police to deal with this case,' the man explained.

'Why not?'

'Well, it would be tantamount of accusing Miss Blane of some more or less criminal action. And if we failed to find anything wrong with her claim, it would lay us open to some considerable unpleasantness from our client.'

'I understand,' agreed Doctor Morelle.

'But, all the same, you think that she is up to something pretty fishy?' Miss Frayle said, thinking that it was time that she showed an intelligent interest in what was going on, if only to offset the unfortunate results of her remarks about violets, which the Doctor now appeared to have forgotten, but which, she was sure, were still at the back of his mind, to be produced at a convenient moment in the future.

Halsted considered with care before he replied to this question. Then he said: 'We're not altogether happy about the purchase of her jewels in the first place.'

Doctor Morelle's sense of logic was offended by the way in which these questions and answers were going on. 'First of all,' he said, 'acquaint me with the circumstances under which the gems were lost, if you don't mind, Mr. Halsted. Is there any possible question of theft?'

'Oh no,' Halsted said. 'That has never been suggested, I think.'

'Well, pray proceed with your account of what happened when the jewels were lost,' Doctor Morelle said.

'The lady is the . . . er . . . ' Halsted hesitated, and then took this hurdle with a jump. 'She is the friend of a certain Baron Roselle,' he said.

'A foreigner?' asked Miss Frayle, reacting as might be expected of her in the circumstances.

'Yes,' Halsted agreed. 'The couple were returning from the Continent, where they had been spending a few weeks' holiday. They crossed by the boat from Dieppe. As they stood on deck, the Baron happened to bump into Miss Blane, who happened at that precise moment to be holding her jewel-case. As a result it was flung from her grasp, went overboard, and is at present at the bottom of the English Channel, somewhere between Dieppe and Newhaven. That, at any rate, is the lady's story of the accident, and I may say that she shows every sign of intending to stick to it.'

'You don't believe it?' Doctor Morelle asked bluntly.

'The whole thing appears to have happened too conveniently,' explained Halsted. 'It is difficult for us to disprove; yet it seems to be such an obvious case for possible fraud that . . . ' His voice trailed away uncertainly, as if he found it not at all easy to put his suspicions into precise words.

'Were there any witnesses to the alleged accident?' Doctor Morelle asked.

'Plenty,' answered Halsted sadly. 'Miss Blane and the Baron are able to call at least four passengers who definitely saw the jewel-case fall into the sea. There is no doubt about that, no doubt at all.'

'And yet you suspect that some act of trickery has taken place?' Doctor Morelle pursued.

'Yes.'

'H'm.' It seemed, for the moment, that Doctor Morelle found the case puzzling even to his superlative analytical intellect. Then he went on: 'You have told me that the — er — lady is in some respects notorious. Have you any reliable information concerning the precise status and ability of her — er — friend, the Baron Roselle?'

'You mean, Doctor, that you think he may be a phoney?' Miss Frayle asked in excited tones.

'Miss Frayle!' exclaimed the Doctor. 'Your Americanisms are truly shocking to the sensitive ear.'

'Oh,' answered Halsted, 'he is a genuine Baron all right. We have had various enquiries made into all that sort of thing. That was the obvious first line of attack.'

'But you still retain certain, possibly ill-defined, suspicions of Miss Blane and the Baron?' Doctor Morelle insisted.

'Yes. You see, we have reason to suppose that they are both pretty hard-up.'

'What caused their state of financial stringency?' Doctor Morelle asked.

'They have extravagant tastes, both of them,' Halsted explained. 'And, I should think that they have been living beyond their incomes for years past.'

Doctor Morelle grinned grimly. 'They would appear to be quite a delectable couple,' he remarked.

'Helen Blane's awfully attractive,' Miss Frayle mused with an air of envy.

'Beauty,' Doctor Morelle snapped at her, 'is only skin deep. That is a fact for which you, my dear Miss Frayle, should be duly grateful!'

Miss Frayle looked somewhat taken aback by this attack. 'When it's too late,' she murmured, 'I expect that I'll think of a suitable answer to that one.'

'What did the precious stones comprise?' Doctor Morelle enquired of Halsted, patiently ignoring Miss Frayle's sotto-voce remark.

'I've got a list of them here,' Halsted said, producing a sheet of paper from his pocket.

'Good,' Doctor Morelle commented. 'Would you read it to me, please?'

Halsted read: 'Diamond and sapphire bracelet, valued at £6,000, pair of ruby earrings, valued £5,000.'

'Is that all?' Doctor Morelle asked.

Halsted smiled. 'There are some smaller items, also an emerald necklace, valued at £10,000. The smaller items are of no real importance; but you will see that when three items total £21,000 the matter is a big thing, even for a company of the size of mine.'

Doctor Morelle again mused. 'Doubtless,' he said, 'you hold the receipts regarding the money which she had paid for those three large items?'

Halsted agreed. 'I've got the receipts with me,' he said. 'Why do you ask?'

'Might I have the opportunity of

perusing them?' Doctor Morelle asked.

Again Halsted fumbled with papers in his pocket, and finally handed over the documents. 'Here they are,' he said. 'They seem to be in order.'

'But you have your doubts?'

'Yes.'

Doctor Morelle took the proffered receipts and examined them with considerable care. Miss Frayle noted that he spread them out on the desk, scanned them rapidly, and then appeared to be comparing the three receipts, as if he anticipated finding some contradictions between them. Miss Frayle was not at all sure what the Doctor expected to find; but she knew that he would inevitably lay his finger on the weak spot of the case, if such a weak spot did, in fact, exist.

'I perceive,' Doctor Morelle remarked, 'that the diamond and sapphire bracelet, the emerald necklace, and the ruby earrings were all purchased by the same firm, though at widely varying dates.'

'Yes.'

'Are you,' the Doctor went on, 'in any way acquainted with this firm?'

'Yes.'

'Have they a good reputation in business circles?'

'Not bad. But it is practically a one-man business,' explained Halsted.

'And who is the individual behind it?' Doctor Morelle asked. Miss Frayle, watching the Doctor's face, felt sure that he had already laid his finger on the vital clue which would soon reveal the solution of the mystery.

'A chap called Thomson,' Halsted said. 'Came to London from Edinburgh about fifteen years ago. He set up in Hatton Garden as a diamond merchant, and afterwards he opened a retail shop in Bond Street — the shop where Miss Blane bought these jewels. I've had his business connections pretty closely investigated, and there's virtually nothing against him. If there is some sort of fraud involved in this affair, it will be the first time that anything of the kind has been alleged against him. I've been pretty discreet in my enquiries, but I think that I can safely say that nothing criminal has ever been brought home to him — or, for that matter, ever suspected.'

'But in spite of that,' persisted Doctor Morelle, 'you still suspect this individual of being in some way implicated with this woman and her companion?'

Halsted hesitated before replying, as if he found the whole business infinitely distasteful. 'Yes,' he answered at length, 'I suspect that there is something queer about the receipts. But without some sort of proof I'm stuck. And my reason for coming to you is that I thought you might be able to do something in the way of supplying that proof.'

Doctor Morelle looked at his secretary. 'Miss Frayle!' he snapped sharply.

'Yes, Doctor?'

'Have your notebook handy, please, if you will be so kind.'

'Certainly, Doctor.' Miss Frayle was gently surprised at this request, but she always tried very hard not to reveal any kind of astonishment at whatever Doctor Morelle might show himself disposed to do. From long experience she knew only too well that the Doctor's actions, however incomprehensible they might appear to be on the surface, had a way of turning out in the end to be sensible and capable of leading to satisfactory results.

'Will you kindly note down the details of the receipts which Mr. Halsted has given me?'

'Certainly, Doctor Morelle.' Miss Frayle had her pencil poised at the 'ready'.

'One diamond and sapphire bracelet,' Doctor Morelle read, 'purchased October 15, 1938.'

Miss Frayle scribbled hurriedly. 'One diamond and sapphire bracelet,' she repeated slowly, 'purchased October 15, 1938.'

Doctor Morelle looked annoyed. 'If you could possibly refrain from repeating it aloud after me!' he snapped. 'Just content yourself with writing it down as accurately as possible, if you do not mind.'

'Yes, Doctor Morelle,' said Miss Frayle meekly. Halsted looked gently surprised at the quiet way in which she took this rebuke. But he did not know the long course of training that Miss Frayle had undergone in order to reach this state of meekness.

'Emerald necklace,' Doctor Morelle went on, picking up the second receipt, 'purchased July 23, 1943. Have you got that down, Miss Frayle?'

'Yes, Doctor.'

'And finally,' said the Doctor, 'pair of ruby earrings, purchased December 18, 1946. Have you got all those details down, Miss Frayle?'

'Yes, Doctor. But . . . Dr. Morelle . . . ' Miss Frayle was clearly seething with intense excitement, a state in which Doctor Morelle always disliked seeing her. He was wont to say that in such a condition Miss Frayle was the most impossible guide to logical thought which it was possible to imagine. And possibly he was right.

'A moment, Miss Frayle, please,' he said, dismissing her excitement with a wave of the hand. 'Mr. Halsted,' he went on, turning to the insurance man, 'you observe nothing wrong with those receipts?'

'They seem clear and above-board to

me,' Halsted admitted, wondering just what was the point to which the Doctor wished him to direct his attention.

'Are you certain about that?'

'Absolutely. The signature is Thomson's all right. I've taken the trouble to have that investigated,' explained Halsted. 'I've compared those signatures with literally dozens of genuine signatures of the man, and there can, I think, be no doubt that these are absolutely genuine.'

'Yes?' The rise in Doctor Morelle's eyebrows, and the inflexion of his voice suggested that he was still not altogether satisfied by the insurance man's reaction to the questions that were being put to him.

'There's nothing odd about the three twopenny stamps, either,' Halsted went on. 'No; I can't for the life of me see that there is any chance of disputing the reality of those receipts. And if we can't dispute the reality of those receipts, I don't see that there is any chance at all of getting away with the case. It may be Miss Blane, the Baron, and Thomson are all in this together, but I fail to see what chance we have got of proving it. That, indeed, is why I came to you in the first instance, Doctor, hoping that you would be able to see a loophole where — quite frankly — I can see none at all.'

Doctor Morelle smiled grimly. 'Well, Mr. Halsted,' he said, 'in that case, I suppose it might be considered an advantageous stroke of policy to hear just what it is that Miss Frayle has so obviously been bursting to tell us for the past five minutes.'

Miss Frayle, however, no longer appeared to be quite so anxious to dispense information as she had been a bit earlier. She hesitated and then muttered various things, which the Doctor found quite impossible to comprehend.

'Will you be so kind as to explain precisely what you are endeavouring to tell us, Miss Frayle?' he said in his most irritated tones.

'I've got a definite feeling, Doctor,' Miss Frayle began, only to be almost immediately interrupted by her employer.

'I think,' he said, 'that we might leave your intuitive inspirations out of the case,

Miss Frayle. All that I have asked you for and all that I require at the present juncture, is your opinion of the facts in front of you.'

Miss Frayle smiled. 'The facts don't seem to be at all in dispute, Doctor,' she said.

'No?' There was an air of healthy scepticism about the Doctor's voice, which did not altogether escape Miss Frayle's attention, so that she felt that she must do her best to justify what she had been saying, and do it without in any way appearing to be making more excuses.

'Well,' she said. 'I can't see that there is anything wrong with the receipts, of course.'

'No?' Again there was that sceptical monosyllable, which Miss Frayle found so extremely irritating and at the same time almost menacing in its implications.

'No,' she said. 'Mr. Halsted has assured us that he has no doubt that the three signatures are genuine. The stamps are all right — they're all alike — and I can't see that anyone could suggest that there is

187

anything in any way illegal or irregular about the three receipts.'

'No?' Doctor Morelle queried for the third time. 'Then in that case, my dear Miss Frayle, might I perhaps be so bold as to enquire precisely what important information it was that you were so keen to impart to us a few minutes ago when I was engaged in obtaining from Mr. Halsted, facts which, in my own humble opinion, were more directly germane to the issue which we are at present trying to bring to a successful conclusion.'

'My intuition,' Miss Frayle said, albeit rather hesitatingly, 'tells me that no woman with red hair could possibly . . .'

Doctor Morelle's face became furious with anger. 'The colour of her hair, Miss Frayle,' he snapped, 'has nothing whatever to do with the case. On the other hand, there are facts that have to be borne in mind, and which undoubtedly point to . . .'

It was now Halsted's turn to interrupt. 'Something tells me, Doctor,' he said, 'that you have some suspicions about the woman, all the same.'

'I have no suspicions,' Doctor Morelle said firmly.

'But, surely, Doctor,' Miss Frayle said, and then, catching a glimpse of his expression, she came to a halt. It was unwise she knew, to 'bait' him too far. And she knew now that the point of explosion was not very far away.

'I did not suspect,' the Doctor repeated. 'When a case reaches the stage now reached in this one, I never suspect. I *know*.'

'You know?' Halsted could scarcely believe his ears. 'You mean to say, Doctor Morelle, that you know what has been going on in this affair?'

Doctor Morelle nodded somewhat morosely. 'Yes, Mr. Halsted,' he said. 'I know that this is a palpable conspiracy to defraud your firm, carried out by the three individuals whose names you mentioned earlier.'

'You mean that, Doctor?' Halsted said.

'Mr. Halsted, I am not in the habit of making bland assertions which I cannot support by undoubted facts. I can assure you,' the Doctor said, 'that if you will communicate with the police you will not have to pay the thousands of pounds claimed by the lady in the case, but that the police will undoubtedly have the pleasure of a successful prosecution for fraud and conspiracy against the three people whose nefarious activities we have been discussing for the past half-hour or so.'

'Well,' said Miss Frayle, 'it would seem that the feminine intuition which you look at so scornfully, Doctor is not so far off the mark, after all.'

Doctor Morelle's eyes flashed utter contempt. 'My dear Miss Frayle,' he said, 'when the criminals are apprehended, which they will be as soon as Mr. Halsted has the opportunity of communicating with the police, it will be as the result of my own logical deduction, and not as the result of any brilliant strokes of intuition by yourself.'

Miss Frayle smiled. 'Of course, Doctor,' she said, 'I know that those people must have made some dreadful mistake which you were at once able to pounce upon like a cat on a mouse.'

'I was not aware,' commented Doctor

Morelle icily, 'that my characteristics were so notably feline.'

'I'm so sorry, Doctor,' apologised Miss Frayle, 'but I think that you know what I mean.'

'I know one thing, at any rate,' the Doctor remarked.

'And that is?' Halsted said. The insurance man had listened to this exchange of compliments with some amusement; but he thought that it was time that the conversation was brought back to the right lines, since he was extremely anxious to know just what had gone on, the method by which Doctor Morelle had arrived at the conclusion that a definite act of fraud had been carried out by the three conspirators.

'That is that Miss Frayle held the vital clue under her very nose, yet failed to appreciate its real significance, in spite of all that feminine intuition to which she appears to attach so much value and importance . . . '

'Well, I am a bit short-sighted, you know, Doctor,' Miss Frayle retorted.

'Nonsense!' snapped the Doctor. 'Even

at this moment I am sure that you have not the slightest idea of the clue to which I have been referring.'

'That's true; I haven't,' admitted Miss Frayle sadly.

'You observed clearly, in spite of your astigmatism, that the receipts were all in perfect order,' the Doctor pointed out.

'Yes,' Miss Frayle said. 'The signatures and the stamps were exactly the same in the three cases.'

'Precisely!' The Doctor glared round him with an air of positive triumph. 'And that,' he cackled, 'is why I say that I know with absolute certainty that there was a conspiracy to defraud the insurance company on the part of the three individuals whose abilities and activities we have been discussing this morning.'

'But I still don't see,' Miss Frayle began, only once more to be interrupted by the Doctor.

'The stamps were exactly the same,' he said. 'That is the vital clue, Miss Frayle, the precise significance of which so curiously eluded you.'

'But surely, Doctor,' Mr. Halsted said,

his brow wrinkled in bewilderment, 'it would be anticipated that the stamps would be the same. Three twopenny stamps, all during the reign of our present king, would naturally be alike.'

'The stamp dated October 15, 1938, would, in actual fact, have been a quite different shade from the other two,' the Doctor pointed out calmly.

'Really, Doctor?' Miss Frayle said.

'Yes, Miss Frayle,' explained the Doctor. 'The shade of stamps was altered in 1941. That was a wartime measure, which was introduced, I understand, in order to save the dye, which was in the ink. The receipt, dated 1938, should have borne a stamp of a much deeper orange colour than the two that bore later dates. In court, it would be totally impossible for any counsel to oppose that fact. It would be sufficient of itself to prove that the whole affair was based on forged receipts. And, when once that fact had been established, the whole case is naturally worked out to an inexorable and completely logical conclusion.'

'That's brilliant, Doctor,' Halsted said.

'I'm sure that my directors will be immensely obliged to you for so neatly putting your finger on the really crucial clue in this very difficult affair.'

For once, however, Miss Frayle proved to be irrepressible.

'Of course, Doctor,' she said, 'you spotted a very important point.'

'That is extremely kind of you,' Miss Frayle,' he said with a sarcastic smile. 'It is good for you to let me know that what I do meets with your unqualified approval.'

'But I still think,' she went on, 'that my clue, actually, was just as good as yours; and it was one which you didn't mention, and which it is just possible you didn't notice.'

Doctor Morelle's voice took on a harsher tone than usual. 'I can hardly contain my impatience to hear this marvellous clue which you have hit upon, no doubt with the aid of your celebrated intuition Miss Frayle,' he said.

'No woman with flaming red hair would spend thousands of pounds to buy a pair of ruby earrings,' Miss Frayle explained. 'I mean to say, think of the clash of colour. Think of how dreadful they would look against her hair.'

For once Miss Frayle had the unaccustomed pleasure of seeing Doctor Morelle completely taken aback, 'Well, I . . . I . . . ' he stuttered. 'That is to say, that I . . . I . . . '

And Miss Frayle could not resist her little moment of complete triumph. 'Yes, Doctor,' she said, 'you know, you did miss that clue altogether! And I do believe that you're going slightly ruby red in the face yourself!'

THE END

DR. MORELLE MEETS MURDER
A CASE FOR DR. MORELLE
DR. MORELLE'S CASEBOOK
DR. MORELLE INVESTIGATES
DR. MORELLE INTERVENES
SEND FOR DR. MORELLE
DR. MORELLE ELUCIDATES
DR. MORELLE MARCHES ON
MEET JIMMY STRANGE
ENTER JIMMY STRANGE
DEPARTMENT OF SPOOKS

We do hope that you have enjoyed reading this large print book.

Did you know that all of our titles are available for purchase?

We publish a wide range of high quality large print books including:
Romances, Mysteries, Classics
General Fiction
Non Fiction and Westerns

Special interest titles available in large print are:
The Little Oxford Dictionary
Music Book, Song Book
Hymn Book, Service Book

Also available from us courtesy of Oxford University Press:
Young Readers' Dictionary
(large print edition)
Young Readers' Thesaurus
(large print edition)

For further information or a free brochure, please contact us at:
Ulverscroft Large Print Books Ltd.,
The Green, Bradgate Road, Anstey,
Leicester, LE7 7FU, England.
Tel: (00 44) 0116 236 4325
Fax: (00 44) 0116 234 0205

Other titles in the
Linford Mystery Library:

SERPENT'S TOOTH

Michael R. Collings

Eric Johansson lives in Fox Creek with his elderly grandmother. But young Carver Ellis discovers him dead in his bed, having been severely beaten. Then, unfortunately for Ellis, the police officer arrives on the scene already convinced that Ellis murdered the victim. Victoria Sears, and her friend down-mountain, Lynn Hanson, work with Deputy Richard Wroten to clear Ellis and uncover why Johansson died. Can they do it before a crucial piece of evidence disappears?

BLACKOUT!

Steve Hayes and David Whitehead

When Diana Callan was beaten to death, all the evidence suggested that her husband, former Green Beret Christopher Callan, was the killer. He had returned from Afghanistan and developed violent blackouts, during which he could remember nothing. But another suspect was in the frame and if Chris could provide enough evidence to prove his innocence the real murderer could be punished. However, that was easier said than done ... especially while Chris was involved with the girlfriend of a psychotic hoodlum.

THE KILL DOG

John Burke

Maggie is in Prague on a Market Research project. But when a Russian tank rolls up outside her hotel, dashing all her plans, she decides to face the country's menacing and violent situation and drive towards the border. On the way, she acquires a passenger — a fugitive. Jan is a Czech archaeologist, carrying a valuable secret, ignorant of its significance or value. But when he eventually faces his enemies in Czechoslovakia, events prove more dramatic than he'd ever anticipated.

THE ENIGMAS OF
HUGO LACKLAN

John Light

In *The Enigmas of Hugo Lacklan*, Alexander Dunkley relates some of the puzzling anecdotes of his social anthropologist friend. Though quite unacademic, these questions, and others, intrigue Hugo. In *The Vanishing Punk*, how did the punk thief vanish after his crimes? And we can only wonder what the reason was for the odd behaviour of the *Five Elderly Gentlemen*. Then, in *The Expensive Daub*, why were hideous daubs selling for such high prices from a London gallery?